Love MEANS MORE

A GOOD BAD IDEA NOVEL

ARIELLA ZELLE

Dedication

For all of my new readers who embraced this Good Bad Idea.

Author's Note

The **Good Bad Idea** series can be read in any order. However, if you would like to see where Ambrose and Augie's story began, please refer to Chapter 8 of **Bet on Love**.

Welcome to Sunnyside!

Immerse yourself in the world of interconnected series set in the fictional town of Sunnyside

Full of cute sweetness and sexy fun, every story ends with a satisfying HEA and no cliffhangers. Since all of the following series are set in the same town, you can expect to see cameos of your favorite characters! The books are funny, steamy, and can be read in any order.

To access the Sunnyside universe reading order guide, please visit www.ariellazoelle.com/sunnyside

Chapter One

AUGIE

AMBROSE'S VOICE cut through my distraction. "Do you think Rhys and Lucien are fucking?"

Every time he said the word "fucking" in that wonderful Irish brogue of his, it triggered arousing fantasies in my imagination. Unfortunately for me, "fuck" was his favorite word, which meant I got bombarded regularly with sexually stimulating scenarios. I imagined him taking me from behind against our hotel room window while I looked down at the glittering lights of the Vegas strip.

But it was an impossible dream. And people wondered why I was always in a bad mood these days. Almost a decade of pining for someone you couldn't have would do that to a man.

I pulled myself away from my dreams to answer him. "They had to meet Lucien's parents at six o'clock and we left at about five forty-five, so I doubt it. You know what a stickler Lucien is about punctuality."

"No, I meant in general."

"Why do you care?" I asked, sounding sulkier than I intended. I hated being envious that our friends had the chance to work out all their pent-up sexual chemistry in bed after eloping the night before. I'd never be that lucky. The unfairness of it burned me to my core.

Ambrose shrugged his broad shoulders. "I don't."

"So why are we talking about it?"

He frowned at my reaction. It didn't make him any less gorgeous. He was devastatingly handsome, with a strong jaw and killer cheekbones. Combined with his luscious auburn hair, blue eyes, and sexy accent, he was irresistible. He made jeans and a simple black button-down shirt look runway-worthy. Why did he have to be so damn hot?

I despised myself for wanting him so much. Ambrose was an unrepentant flirt, but there was more to him than that. It was the real side of him he only shared with me that kept me lingering in lovesickness all these years. Everything would be infinitely easier if he acted like a dick all the time. Maybe then I wouldn't be so in love with him.

My attention returned to the present when he said with a shrug, "I don't know. Them eloping makes you think is all."

"Think about them fucking?"

He laughed, a rich sound that sent shivers down my spine. "They're straight, so it's a fair question to ask now that they're married."

"It's not really ours to ask, though. That's between them." I tried not to feel the burn of jealousy that our friends had eloped before Rhys made a huge mistake by marrying his awful fiancée.

Ambrose drank his beer before responding. "It just makes me wonder, you know?"

"About what?" I wasn't sure what he was driving at with his cryptic comments.

"What it's like," he replied, but it clarified nothing. "It'd be like me waking up married to you."

The concept was more appealing than I was comfortable with, but I put on my best poker face. "And?"

"We've all joked about Rhys and Lucien being an old married couple for as long as we've known them," he explained. "Now they're married for real, but they're both straight. How does that work?"

Although I knew the conversation would burn me, I played with fire. "What would you do if you woke up and discovered you were my husband?"

His grin was wicked and seductive. "I suppose it depends on how drunk I was from the night before."

I swallowed hard. "Meaning?"

He winked at me, flustering me further. "You know exactly what I mean."

Unprepared to hear there was even the slightest

chance Ambrose would have sex with me under the right circumstances, I could only arch my eyebrows in response.

"You'd have to be willing, of course," he added, a playful twinkle in his eye.

How did this beautiful idiot not understand I'd let him bend me over the table that very minute and take me hard while everyone watched? I continued playing devil's advocate. "Let's say I was willing and eager. What then?"

He almost appeared to be blushing, which was unusual for him when he didn't have a shy bone in his body. There was a lengthy pause before he answered, "I'll try anything once."

It was a testament to my willpower that I didn't volunteer we go upstairs to our room and give it a shot. I deserved an award for restraining myself to a smirk. "Good to know."

"Would you be fine with it?"

I wanted to answer by sweeping everything off the table and spreading my legs for him, but I kept the banter light-hearted and used his own words against him. "I'll try anything once."

"Perhaps if I kick back enough of these, we can get ourselves into some fun trouble tonight." Ambrose raised his beer mug in a toast to me.

Great, that was a new thought to torture myself with for the rest of my life. "Well, the night's still young."

He downed the rest of his drink, making my pants grow tight at the sight of his throat working as he swallowed. His voice had a raw edge to it when he spoke. "'Tis true." His gaze lingered on me, setting my entire body aflame with a lust I tried to hide. "That gives me an idea, actually."

For a fraction of a second, I foolishly hoped he meant we could *finally* end my years of sexual frustration. However, I wasn't nearly that fortunate. "What kind of idea?"

Ambrose glanced over at two stunning women approaching on the way to the bar. He flashed them a charming smile, causing them to giggle as they walked by. Once they were out of earshot, he said, "A fantastic one." The game was on from his excited expression. "I'll be back."

I wanted to tell him not to bother, but he was gone before I could say a word. That left me alone to sit with my confusion about our conversation. Why couldn't Ambrose be serious about wanting to be with me?

Chapter Two

AMBROSE

I HAD ONLY MET one person I couldn't seduce. It was my shite luck that it was who I wanted to be with the most: August Murphy. After a lifetime of pursuing women, I had been in deep denial about my feelings for him for a long time. But it eventually reached a level where I could no longer deny I had fallen for my best friend. It was stupid to want someone I could never have, but I loved him so damn much it hurt.

In the privacy of my mind, August was my Augie, my darlin', the love of my life who loved me back. There had been more than one occasion where I'd almost slipped and used my term of endearment for him in real life, but so far, I had kept my secrets.

I tried openly flirting with him and with other men recently, hoping Augie would take the hint I was open to being with him to no avail. My attempts at making him jealous with other women hadn't worked, either. All I ever seemed to do these days was piss him off at every turn. It frustrated the hell out of me. Was it too much to ask for the greatest love of my life to want me?

Rhys eloping with Lucien granted me the unexpected gift of talking with Augie about exploring a new sexual dynamic in our friendship. But I had completely botched it by getting scared of rejection and implying I would only be with him if I got effing and blinding drunk. It had been the perfect chance to confess I ached to be with him, but I blew it like the biggest moron in the entire world.

The gorgeous women walking by our table arm in arm had been fortuitous. If I couldn't have him, at least I could have the decency to get us both laid. The sexual frustration was driving me crazy, especially because I hadn't hooked up with any of the ladies on this trip like he thought. My longing for him kept interfering with my casual relationships to the point where I had all but stopped sleeping around. I wasn't even interested in these two, but they presented an opportunity for me to be with Augie as part of a group thing. It was a long shot, but if they were present, maybe he would let me kiss him to show off for them. *Fuck, I'm getting desperate.*

I made my way over to the bar, standing near where the two women sat. They were both bombshells in flashy sequin and glitter dresses, one brunette and the other a redhead. With my most charming grin and laying on my accent thick, I greeted them, "Good evening, ladies."

"Hi, handsome," the brunette replied with a friendly smile. "How's your night going?"

"Better now that you're both here," I retorted, causing them to laugh.

The redhead teased her friend in a Belfast accent, which differed from my Dublin one. "Twice the Irish in one night? Aren't you a lucky girl?"

"The luckiest." Her brown eyes were bright as she looked me over with an approving gaze. "I'm a sucker for an Irish accent."

"That's an understatement," her friend said with an amused snort.

The brunette smiled at me. "What can I say? I like what I like." She held out her hand. "I'm Sara, and this is Fiona."

"A pleasure to meet you both." I kissed the back of Sara's hand before doing the same to Fiona.

"Are you planning on abandoning your mate?" Fiona asked, tilting her head in Augie's direction.

Even at a distance, he was stunning. His delicate features and gorgeous green eyes never failed to make my heart beat that much faster. He looked amazing in his purple blazer over a pink shirt, paired with skintight white jeans that showed off that pert arse of his I longed for. As always, he styled his dark hair in a perfect pompadour he somehow pulled off without looking ridiculous.

I realized I had gotten sidetracked. "No, I wouldn't dream of it. He's a little shy, so that's why I'd like to ask on his behalf if you ladies would join us on a double date tonight?"

They exchanged a look before Fiona nodded. Sara answered for them, "Sure, that sounds fun!"

After we picked up our drinks, we returned to the table. I sat down next to Augie in the booth, passing him a beer as they took the chairs opposite of us. "These beautiful ladies are Sara and Fiona."

"Nice to meet you. I'm August." His gaze lingered on the redhead, just as I expected. He had probably dated more Irish girls than me. I liked to flatter myself that he preferred them because they resembled me, but it was wishful thinking at best. "What brings you to Vegas?"

"Our friend is getting married tomorrow," Sara explained. "We're in the bridal party."

"We were supposed to be groomsmen in our friend's wedding, but he eloped with his best man yesterday," I said. It was weird being envious of Lucien and Rhys's rash decision. "That leaves us free to have our fun tonight."

"Running off with your best man?" Fiona sipped her martini. "How very Vegas of them."

"It's more romantic than it sounds." Augie's word choice surprised me. "They're childhood best friends who were finally honest with themselves about how they felt for each other. Walking down the aisle with his fiancée would have been an enormous mistake."

Sara sighed with a dreamy expression on her face. "I'm glad true love won out."

He sounded wistful as he commented, "They're lucky."

Sara looked at Augie as she asked, "I'd say we're the lucky ones, wouldn't you?"

He tilted his head in confusion. "I'm not sure I know what you mean."

"Oh, come on. Yes, you do." She gave him a knowing look. "Nothing makes my panties come off faster than someone who is gorgeous and has a thick Irish brogue. There's no way I'm the only person at this table with that tendency."

"I think you mean fetish," Fiona corrected her with a roguish grin.

Augie's cheeks tinged pink as his gaze darted over to me and away again. Whenever he did things like that, I wondered if I might have a realistic chance with him after all. "Thank god it's not just me for once."

The women cracked up with peals of laughter, while I grew distracted by a mental image of him wearing a pair of black lace panties. It aroused me before I could stop it. I took a swig of my beer to drown out that thought. It wasn't the time or place for that kind of thing, even if it was sexy as sin. That was something to add to the wank bank to enjoy much later when I was by myself.

Fiona winked at me. "That must be useful for getting anything you want, eh?"

"Occasionally." I had seduced countless women with my accent alone, but it hadn't helped me win the affections of the only person I craved. It was hard not to feel disheartened sometimes.

"He's being modest," Augie told her, before adding, "which is a rarity."

"How long have you been together?"

Her phrasing was odd, but I didn't comment on it. "We met our freshman year of college, and we've been inseparable ever since."

Sara held her hand over her heart. "That's so romantic!"

"Is it?" It seemed like a strange choice of word to describe our friendship.

"I've always thought there's something extra romantic about being in love with your best friend. It's the best feeling in the universe." As she beamed at Fiona with affection, it was my first real clue that I may have misjudged the situation. "Right, Fi?"

"Absolutely." Fiona's fondness for Sara was obvious.

Without meaning to, I added, "Only when you're lucky enough that they love you back."

Augie stared at me with a puzzled look but startled when his phone rang. I glanced over at his screen and saw it was his younger brother calling. "Sorry, I have to take this."

I frowned as he rushed toward the restrooms alcove to answer the call. If Felix was calling, there was a disaster in the making somewhere. I adored the kid like my own brother, but he had the worst timing sometimes.

"Is everything okay?" Sara asked in a worried tone.

"I hope so," I answered, feeling uneasy. "His younger brother only calls when something is wrong. The last time Felix called, he was at the hospital after his car accident."

"Oh no, that's terrible! Here's hoping it's nothing serious this time." Her genuine concern was touching. She seemed like such a sweet girl. Too bad I only had eyes for Augie.

I glanced back over to where Augie had gone, but he stood behind the wall. After their mom passed away when they were young, he had raised his younger brother while their dad grieved. His protective need to take care of Felix had put him in a tough position more than once. I hoped that wouldn't be the case tonight. "Would you mind if I go check on him?"

"Not at all."

"Your boyfriend is way more of a priority," Sara added. "We'll get another round of drinks for everyone while we wait, okay?"

Her description of Augie confirmed my suspicion

that they had misunderstood what I meant by the term "double date." It gave me an idea, but I doubted that he would play along. If everything was fine with Felix, I'd try to persuade him to come around to my plan. I would be in for the best night of my life if I could get him to agree.

With a word of thanks to them, I left to go talk to him.

Chapter Three

AUGIE

MY HEART WAS in my throat as I answered my younger brother's call. I didn't bother with a greeting. "What's wrong?"

"I'm so stupid," Felix whispered, his voice thick with tears.

That certainly didn't narrow down the options. "I need you to be more specific than that."

He sniffled with a miserable noise. "You warned me, but I didn't listen."

That could only mean one thing: something had happened with his asshole boyfriend, who I had cautioned him repeatedly not to date. I held in a sigh as I asked in a resigned tone, "What did Danny do?"

My younger brother started crying. "I found out he cheated on me, so he broke up with me when I confronted him about it."

I winced at the inevitable conclusion of their relationship. It wasn't surprising, but it sucked all the same. "I'm sorry, Felix."

"Why are you sorry? You're the one who told me this would happen. I should have listened to you. This is all my fault."

"No, it's his for being a cheating piece of shit," I corrected him. "You did nothing wrong."

"I loved him."

It broke my heart to hear how miserable he was. I checked my watch for the time. "I'm not sure if I can catch a flight home tonight, but—"

"No, please don't come back early," he pleaded. "That'll make me feel even worse. That's not why I called you."

"You shouldn't be alone right now."

"It's more important for you to be there for Rhys's wedding."

In all the excitement, I realized I forgot to tell him about what had happened. "There is no wedding."

"What?"

"Rhys eloped with Lucien last night. The wedding with Olivia is off."

There was a stunned silence on the other end. "No shit, really?"

"Yep, they got married at an Elvis chapel after the bachelor party yesterday."

"Good for them. Too bad I'll never know what that's like."

I refocused his attention. "Look, I'm out with Ambrose, but I'll head back to our room and—"

Felix groaned. "Please don't. I won't forgive myself if you do that."

"But—"

"I'm begging you not to cut your trip short. You should make the most of your time together with Ambrose."

My brother knew better than anyone about my complicated feelings for my best friend. "It's not like that." That was the problem—it would never be like that. I started to say something further, but the man in question came around the corner. I changed topics to a more pressing issue. "If you don't want to stay with Dad, you can stay with me as long as you need to."

"The only good thing is he felt guilty enough for cheating that he agreed to go to his brother's place for a week while I move out. I'm sure I can find a new apartment before then. Thanks, though."

"If you can't, I always have room for you."

He sniffled again. "Thank you."

There were few things I hated more than being helpless to do anything for him. "I honestly don't mind coming back to be with you."

"No, I'll call my friends Wren and Izzy and hang out with them until you return, okay? That way I won't be alone, and you won't have to worry about me."

"I always worry about you."

He sighed. "I know, but please promise me you won't fly back here early because I'm a dumbass."

It went against my nature not to be there for Felix when he was going through a hardship. But as Ambrose stood nearby and watched with concern, my resolve wavered. "Only if that's what you want."

"What I really want is for you two to take a cue from Rhys and Lucien and admit you have feelings for each other. At least one of us should be happy and loved."

I said his name but wasn't certain what I was trying to express. Being so far away made me feel useless.

"Ambrose is there, isn't he?" he asked.

"Yeah."

"Give the phone to him."

I could only imagine the things he would say to my best friend. "Absolutely not."

"Please?"

When Felix used that pleading tone of voice with me, I could never say no. With a heavy sigh, I held my phone out to my best friend.

Ambrose took it from me with a questioning expression. "What happened?" He was silent while Felix filled him in on the breakup. "Damn, that sucks, Felix. We can be on the next plane if—"

My heart twisted in my chest at Ambrose's willingness to leave Vegas with me to go take care of my brother. That was the side of him I loved more than anything. He always came through for me when it mattered most. Some of my ex-girlfriends had hated how devoted I was to Felix, but Ambrose understood why. It helped that he had a younger brother, Callum, whom he was extremely close to. He would do anything for his brother, so he never resented me for being that way. Ambrose was like a second big brother to Felix, which meant the world to me.

I wasn't sure what Felix said to interrupt Ambrose, but both of his eyebrows flew up in surprise at whatever it was. "Uh, that's—I'll see what I can come up with. But in return, promise me you'll manage until we get back, okay? You know August will worry himself to death about you otherwise." He nodded at my brother's response. "Good lad. Take care of yourself, you hear me? Here's your brother." He passed the phone back to me.

Before I could ask what he had said to Ambrose, Felix informed me, "I suggested he tie you up in bed to make you stay there."

I pressed my palm against my forehead as I tried to rein in my urge to thump my brother through the phone. "Thanks for that."

"Thank me after he wears you out with the best sex of your life." He sounded more like himself, which helped ease my guilt about not being there for him. "I'll be fine, August. I promise."

"If you need anything, call me, okay? I don't care what time it is."

"Thanks. I'll talk to you when you get back."

As soon as I hung up, Ambrose gathered me into a tight hug. I clung to him, savoring being safe in his strong arms. He smelled like teakwood and vanilla, comforting me even while tantalizing my senses. For that one moment, I had everything I desired.

His voice was gentle as he offered, "If we need to go—"

I shook my head no. That would mean leaving his embrace. I lingered for a little longer, not ready to give up the comfort of being held by him. "I promised him I wouldn't come home early."

He stepped back but didn't release me. "Are you okay with that, though?"

Whenever he looked at me with those beautiful blue eyes full of concern, I fell in love with him all over again. "Honestly? No. But he insisted he wants me to stay here, so I'll respect that. It helps to know he'll be with Wren and Izzy. They're good friends."

Ambrose finally let go of me. I immediately mourned the loss of his body against mine. He ran his fingers through his hair as he said, "Speaking of good friends."

"Yes?"

"The girls think we're more than good friends. They think we're boyfriends. And I'm pretty sure they're girlfriends."

I didn't know what I should do with that information. "So, you want to bail?"

Ambrose shook his head. "No, I think we still have a chance."

It went without saying, but I said it anyway. "I doubt it. If they're lesbians, they're definitely not interested in us."

"Sara seems really into me. Maybe they're bi and looking to swing?"

"I doubt that."

"What's the harm in seeing where it goes? We should lean into it and give it a go."

I looked at him quizzically. "Are you suggesting you'll pretend to be my boyfriend so you can get with Sara?"

"And you can hook up with Fi," he added. "This isn't only about me."

Fiona was gorgeous and her accent was to die for, but the only Irish person I lusted after was Ambrose. "Doesn't that make you uncomfortable?"

He shrugged. "Not really. It's not like it would be my first time."

His comment baffled me. "Not your first time doing what?"

"Hooking up with multiple people at the same time."

It took a second for the full implications of his comment to process for me. "Wait, are you saying you want to be with me at the same time as them?" The thought was almost more than I could handle. "As in actually *be with me* and not just them?"

"It's Vegas," he said, acting like that explained everything. "Why not?"

Part of me was more than ready to jump on the too-good-to-be-true offer, but the rest of me was in too much disbelief to accept so easily. "You can't possibly be serious about this. You're not into guys." That was when something occurred to me that turned my stomach. "Wait, when you said you had been with multiple people at the same time, did that include men?"

I needed him to say no, because I didn't know how to deal with him answering yes. The idea that he had been indulging in sex orgies with men that weren't me was too much to bear. If he had, that would mean it wasn't my dick that put him off, it was me as a person. I wasn't prepared to deal with that kind of crushing rejection at the moment, or ever if I was being honest.

"No, there were never men involved," he answered, causing me to breathe a sigh of relief. "This is different, though. You're my best friend."

"That doesn't mean that you want to—" I cut myself off when a man walked past us to go into the bathroom. Only once I was sure we were alone again did I lower my voice to a whisper to finish my sentence. "That doesn't mean you want to fuck me."

"What happened to being willing and eager?" He smirked in a way that reduced me to a puddle. "Was that all just talk earlier?"

"I didn't think you were serious!"

His blue eyes burned with challenge, daring me to accept what I had spent almost a decade longing for. "As you said, the night's still young. Let's see where it takes us."

I wished I was brave enough to suggest that we forget about the woman and go upstairs by ourselves, but I couldn't make myself say it. Getting shot down would hurt too much. "This bad idea will backfire on us, you know that, right?"

"Come on, it'll distract you from worrying about your brother and get you laid at the same time. It's a win-win. What's wrong with a little make-believe?"

My gut told me I should bail before he broke my heart, but my morbid curiosity about what Ambrose would do defeated my common sense. Even if it was only pretending for one night, I wanted him to be mine. "Fine. If you're that interested in being my fake boyfriend, who am I to say no?"

"I'M sorry that took so long," I apologized once we returned to the table where the women waited.

"Is your brother okay?" Sara asked with worry.

"He will be. His boyfriend cheated on him and then dumped him when he found out, so he was upset."

Fiona wrinkled her nose in disgust. "What a piece of shite. Your brother's better off without him."

"Agreed," Ambrose said. I tensed when he reached his arm out along the back of the booth to rub my shoulder in comfort but quickly relaxed into his touch. "Felix is a good lad. He deserves better."

"He deserves the happiness you two have." Sara picked up her martini glass and held it in a toast. "Here's to him finding his true love like us."

We all lifted our drinks to cheer to that, although it hurt knowing I'd never be lucky enough to have that kind of love with Ambrose for real.

"How did you two meet?" Ambrose asked them.

Sara lit up at the question. "We met at a dog park. I was instantly smitten, so I offered to be her dog walker when she went back to Ireland to visit her family. When Fi returned, I was determined to make her mine."

"Sadly, I had some Catholic guilt I had to work through before I was comfortable enough to be with her." Fiona shook her head. "My sole regret is it took me so long to come to terms with my feelings for her."

"Same." I glanced over at him in surprise at his commiseration with her. "Thankfully, Augie was willing to wait for me to sort through all of my bullshit."

I shot him a look. *Augie?* Since when had he ever called me that? And why did it send tingles down my spine?

Sara squealed in delight. "Oh, that's such a cute nickname!"

She was right, but it was also a little embarrassing. How had he come up with that so fast? Distracted, it took me a moment to get back on track with playing into the fantasy. "I had been pining for him for years, so I was good at waiting by that point. It was totally worth it to be with him finally." *Oh, if only.*

Sara smiled at Fiona, radiating love for her. "I would have waited a hundred years if that's what it took to be with her."

"Thankfully, I had the good sense not to make you wait *that* long," Fiona said. "I'll always be grateful that Brett helped me get my head out of my arse."

Sara grinned. "Brett was an ex-boyfriend of mine who was trying to reconnect with me. I wasn't interested in him at all, but she didn't know that."

"I thought the only way I could stop her from going back to him was to be with me. It gave me the courage I needed to make my move."

Ambrose moved his hand to stroke the nape of my neck with his thumb. It sent shivers of lust racing through me. "Huh, maybe it's an Irish thing. I finally acknowledged my feelings for Augie when I got jealous seeing him with a woman."

He was lying, but it didn't stop me from adding a truthful statement. "I was only with her because I couldn't have you."

Sara gave me a sympathetic look. "I always thought that would make it better, but it never did."

"No, it really didn't." I tried not to get choked up over how understanding she was about my plight. "It just made it worse."

"Thankfully, those days are behind us. I have the rest of our lives to make it up to you." He took my hand in his and brought it up to press a tender kiss against my knuckles, causing my heart to stutter. Shit, I wasn't going to survive this.

Fiona chuckled at his response. "You seem like quite the romantic."

"Oh, absolutely. After making Augie live with doubt for so long about how I felt about him, I want to make sure he always knows how much I love him now." He smiled at me with an adoration that took my breath away. How could he look at me like he genuinely loved me? And why couldn't it be true? "I think my favorite romantic gesture was the cabin trip."

Sara clasped her hands together as she sighed, "Oh, that sounds so lovely!"

"I'm an IT manager, and we had a major system upgrade that turned into a nightmare disaster. In the process, I inadvertently neglected our relationship because I had to put in so much overtime to fix everything. To apologize, I surprised him with a trip to a cabin in a ski resort town. We curled up under a flannel blanket in front of the fireplace, drinking hot cocoa with Irish whiskey in it, and spent hours catching up with each other. It was heavenly."

My heart ached in my chest. That sounded like everything I had ever wanted and could never have. I also burned with a painful envy, wondering what girl he had taken that trip with to base the story on and why did she get so lucky.

He continued. "We lucked out that there was a snowstorm, so we got snowed in for two extra days. It gave us the chance to reconnect. I promised myself after that I would never let work get in the way of our relationship again."

"Wow, that sounds incredible. Too bad Fi hates the cold."

The corners of Fiona's lips turned upward in a smirk. "Oh, I'm sure I wouldn't complain too much if you found a way to keep me warm."

"I have a few ideas." Sara's cheeks flushed as she gave Fiona a coy smile. "Although, I wouldn't say no to another trip to Aruba. That place was paradise."

"What more can you ask for than a beautiful beach, glorious sunshine, and your sexy lover?"

Before I could second-guess myself, I told a true story. "Your best recent surprise was my twenty-sixth birthday last month."

"Ooh, what did he do?" Sara eagerly asked.

"He said he would take me to my favorite place for dinner. I thought he meant Cavatolli's, which is this amazing Italian restaurant near us. Instead, he took me home to my dad's house to have dinner with him and my brother."

Ambrose added, "Augie had been so busy with his job at the ad agency that it had been a while since he had been home to visit his family. I knew there was nowhere else he'd rather be for his birthday than with them."

"Wow, that's so sweet!"

"It meant everything to me that he understood I'd rather be with Dad and Felix for my birthday instead of eating out at a fancy restaurant. Spending the evening with my three favorite people in the world was the best night I could have asked for." I dared to glance over at Ambrose after my confession, and the loving way he looked at me made it hard to breathe. His affectionate gaze was too much to bear, so I looked away. "Afterward, we stayed up in my room and talked until we fell asleep. It was perfect."

One of the best parts of that birthday had been the morning after. I woke up with Ambrose spooning me from behind, holding me in his muscular arms with his impressive hard-on pressed against my ass. I'd wanted to roll over and take advantage of his morning wood but had restrained myself to rocking back against him. It wrung a delicious moan out of him as he automatically thrust against me, giving me a tantalizing glimpse of what I so desperately wanted.

Unfortunately, he had pulled away from me and skulked to the bathroom to take care of himself. It allowed me the chance to rub a quick one out, but that would not be the last time I jerked off to the memories of that morning. Even remembering it now was turning me on, which was uncomfortable given how tight my white jeans were and I was at a table with three other people.

I had hoped for a repeat experience in Vegas since we shared a hotel room, but Ambrose had ruined my chances of that by staying out with women the past two nights. It was hard not to take the rejection personally.

Ambrose drew my attention back to him when he corrected me, "It was *almost* perfect." I arched an eyebrow at him at the challenge, causing him to grin. "Your brother interrupting us the next day to ask if we wanted sausage for breakfast kind of ruined my morning plans."

I snorted, since that had happened, albeit after Ambrose had returned from taking care of himself in the bathroom.

"At least I got him back by telling him to go away because I was already enjoying my breakfast 'sausage' in bed." My brother had mercilessly teased me about Ambrose's joke for weeks after that.

Everyone laughed, but I had a tough time remembering to do so when the fantasy of Ambrose giving me a blow job in my childhood bedroom played out in my mind. I had to pull myself from the alluring fantasy before my semi turned into a full hard-on.

Sara giggled in delight. "Wow, he walked right into that one, didn't he? He should have stuck with cereal as an option instead."

Fiona gave Ambrose a knowing smirk. "Something tells me you would have no problem turning that into a sexual innuendo."

His smug expression made my pants grow tight enough that I shifted awkwardly on the seat. I had to resist the urge to palm my hardness for some relief as he purred, "It's one of my many charms."

As they continued bantering, I withdrew into myself. I struggled between being incredibly aroused and horribly depressed that none of this was real. My intention to use the girls as an excuse to hook up with Ambrose made me not just an awful friend, but a terrible person. The pessimist in me knew it would devastate me afterward when he realized he hated being with me like that. But at least I would have that one night to get me through the rest of my days of pining away for him. Although, the more likely case was that he would chicken out before things ever got that far. He talked a good game, but I couldn't imagine my straight best friend wanting to go through with it for real.

Ambrose brushed his thumb against my upper arm, bringing me back to the present as it raised cold chills on my skin. Even such a small touch sent an electric jolt through me. "I think we should do something fun to get Augie's mind off Felix. Do you ladies have any suggestions?"

"We were going to check out a club not too far from here," Fiona answered. "You should join us!"

"Yes, you must!" Sara insisted.

Clubs had never been my scene, but the thought of dancing pressed close against Ambrose's perfect body was tempting as hell. But as I looked down at my well-tailored purple blazer over a pink shirt paired with white jeans, I realized it was far from the ideal outfit for the occasion. "I'm not really dressed for it."

Without missing a beat, Ambrose asked, "Since we're staying in this hotel, would you ladies mind if we went upstairs and changed first?"

"Not at all! It'll give us a chance to freshen up in our room, too," Fiona agreed. The sultry wink she gave Sara implied that wouldn't be the only thing they would do as we got ready.

He told me with a shrug, "I'm down for it if you are."

Warning bells went off in my mind about how terrible the idea was, but I didn't listen. If I was going to be his fake boyfriend, I would go all in and take full advantage of it. "Sure, it sounds like fun."

What was the worst that could happen?

Chapter Four

AMBROSE

AFTER THE LADIES got off the elevator on their floor, Augie and I continued up to our room. He remained silent, making me wonder if maybe I had crossed a line and upset him. When he was so withdrawn, getting a read on his mood proved difficult.

Once we were alone in our room, I asked, "What's on your mind?"

He frowned as he seemed to struggle with how to answer my simple question before finally demanding, "Who did you take to the cabin?"

I arched an eyebrow in surprise. Out of all the questions I expected from him, that hadn't been the first one I thought he'd ask. "Nobody."

My answer confounded him. "Who did you want to bring there?"

I was too much of a coward to admit how often I had fantasized about that kind of cozy weekend snowed in with Augie. Instead, I played it off by pushing his buttons. "Jealous?"

He glowered at me, confirming I hit a nerve. "No," he peevishly denied, but I didn't believe him at all. Everything in his agitated countenance indicated that the thought of me having a romantic weekend away with someone bothered him. It further fueled my hopes that maybe he liked me as more than a friend.

I shrugged. "It was just a general idea."

His green gaze pierced right through my bullshite. "I don't believe you. It was way too detailed to be anything other than true."

"I'm hurt you think so little of my imagination." To distract him, I undid my shirt buttons. I smirked when his eyes followed my actions. "I'm curious why that's your main concern."

"It's not," he shot back, even though he couldn't look away when I shrugged out of my shirt. With my chiseled physique on full display, Augie's cheeks grew pink as he drank in the sight of me bare-chested.

I relished his obvious attraction to me. Somehow, I needed to get him to act on it. Deciding to have a little fun, I ran my hand along my abs and up my chest. He couldn't stop watching, which made my ego purr under his undivided attention. "What is?"

He blinked several times as he pulled out of his stupor. "Huh?"

The reaction gratified me. I repeated with emphasis, "What is your main concern?"

Augie glanced away with a scowl before meeting my gaze once more. It sent an electric thrill through me to see the fierce challenge in his eyes. "Why are you so good at pretending to be my boyfriend?"

Truthfully, it was easy to act the part when we had been dating for over two years in our fantasy life inside the privacy of my mind. It wasn't the right time to fess up to that, though. Not wanting to give myself away, I tried to play it cool. "Because it's not really that different from our normal friendship."

"What are you talking about? This is completely different!"

"Is it?"

He took off his purple jacket with an annoyed noise. "It absolutely is."

"If that was true, then why did you bring up your birthday?" I knew I had him when his whole body tensed up at the question. "They obviously thought it was a romantic gesture. It certainly sounded like one in that context." And it had absolutely been my intention, even though he had no clue about it.

Augie avoided looking at me by digging through his luggage for something to change into. "You didn't mean it that way, though. You were just being a good friend." He sighed in irritation. "What the hell am I supposed to wear? I didn't pack anything for clubbing."

Not wanting him to talk himself out of going, I took out a black tank from my suitcase. "It's not like you have to dress up fancy." I put it on, the thin fabric clinging to my defined form and showing off my muscular arms. "You've got to have at least one T-shirt in there that would work."

With a scowl, he grabbed a purple one from his luggage. He said nothing as he stripped out of his pink button-down shirt. I savored the image of him shirtless for as long as it took for him to pull on the purple one. Instead of it being just plain cotton, it was metallic and fit him like a second skin. It paired nicely with his tight white jeans that made his arse even more tempting than it already was.

Wanting to lift his spirits, I teased him, "I love something that flashy is your idea of having nothing to wear out. Why did you even bring that?"

"It was supposed to go with my green jacket during the bachelor party, but I changed my mind." He tugged at the hem of the shirt. "It's weird wearing it by itself."

"You look fabulous, darlin'." I cringed inwardly when I realized I had said the term of endearment out loud. It had been easy to slip up when he looked so good that I didn't want to leave the hotel room.

The pink of his cheeks turned even rosier. "Trust me, nobody will look at me with you dressed like that."

I walked over to him and stepped into his personal

space. He studied me with wide eyes, the perfect picture of innocence. Everything in me wanted to lean down and capture his lush lips in a kiss, but I couldn't. "You're wrong." I tried and failed to resist the urge to caress his cheek. "I won't be able to take my eyes off you."

Flustered, he put some distance between us. He sounded shaky when he told me, "Stop it. You don't have to pretend when they're not here to see."

"Who said I was pretending?" I did my best to act casual as I walked to the door while my heart raced from being so daring. It took him a moment to follow me downstairs to meet the ladies.

As we waited for the elevator to come, he demanded, "Why are you so fine with this?"

"Because it's you."

My answer didn't seem to satisfy him. "Shouldn't you be uncomfortable with this farce?"

The doors opened and we entered the empty elevator to ride down to the lobby to meet Sara and Fiona. I skirted as close as I could to the truth without fully confessing how I felt about Augie. "Why? It's not like I'm lying about you being one of the most important people in my life." When he didn't respond, my stupid gob kept going. "I mean, in some weird way, aren't we basically platonic boyfriends who do everything together but fuck?"

He stared at me in stunned disbelief, unable to formulate a response of any kind. It was completely understandable, given that was a thought I *really* should have kept in my damn head. When would I ever learn?

Then again, if I was already in this deep, I may as well commit. I reached over and took his hand in mine, interlacing our fingers just in time for the elevator doors to open on the ground floor. He said nothing but didn't pull away. I loved the way his smaller hand felt in mine as we walked over to where Sara and Fiona were waiting for us.

"Ready to go have some fun?" Sara asked.

"Lead the way."

WHEN WE ENTERED the nearby nightclub, there was an intense crush of bodies moving in sync to the pounding beat. Fiona and Sara led the way through the crowded dance floor, before they pulled each other close and started sensuously dancing against each other.

The music was so loud you couldn't hear yourself think, let alone talk. It made it easier to fall into the rhythm and forget about everything. The occasion was a perfect excuse to touch Augie like I had been dreaming about for years. I got behind him, pulling him closer by his waist, his back flush against my body as we moved together. When he didn't reject me, my hands roamed all over his torso until I worked up the nerve to slide them under his shirt to caress his bare skin. I was all hard angles, but his softness was divine.

As the songs blended into each other without pause, I lost all sense of time as we danced. Our bodies moved as one with every roll of our hips, arousing me as we continued. Rather than step away to disguise the fact I was getting erect from the experience, I rocked against his tight arse. It gave me all kinds of ideas about what I wanted to do once we got back to our hotel. It should have been scary to let my body confess the truth I had tried to deny for so long, but I felt free.

I caught a glimpse of Fiona behind Sara, lovingly nuzzling her as they danced. If we were to convince them we were an actual couple, that meant playing the part. It was the perfect excuse to do things I had dreamed about for ages. Without hesitation, I licked up the curve of Augie's neck, tasting his sweat we had worked up dancing in the hot club. It made me think of sex in the summer, which was a glorious thought. There was something so natural about my actions, even though we didn't have that kind of relationship.

He reached back with his left hand, threading his fingers through my hair as he inclined his head to give me better access.

Not needing to be told twice, I capitalized on his silent permission. I kissed my way up to his ear before I tugged on the shell with my teeth. He shuddered against me with a gasp which pushed my desires higher, making it impossible to hide the fact that I was fully erect because of how much I wanted him. "Fuck, Augie."

When he started drawing away from me, I reacted on instinct. I caught his wrist and yanked him against my body so we were now face-to-face. He stared up at me with a fiery desire that stole my breath. The greatest shock was he was just as aroused as I was, unbelievable as it was to me.

Our bodies resumed swaying to the driving beat as we moved in a mimicry of fucking that sent my lust skyrocketing. It was so good I forgot about everything else that wasn't his hard cock and hot body pushing me to my limits.

Out of the corner of my eye, I saw Fiona kiss Sara. That looked like a grand idea. My desire made me throw caution to the wind, and I leaned down and captured Augie's lips, delving in deep for a taste of him. It was the hottest kiss of my entire life as I claimed his mouth as mine, more turned on than I had ever been before. His surrender to me made me feel high as I took everything he offered. When I grabbed his arse, he whimpered. I damn near came in my pants from the powerful rush of carnal need that rocketed through my system. It was better than even my best dreams.

We only realized what had happened when we paused for air. A look of horror passed over his face and he bolted before I could stop him. I pursued him without so much as a single backward glance at Fiona or Sara.

AUGIE REFUSED to speak to me until we were back in our hotel room. He kept his distance as he glared at me with a pained betrayal that gutted me. I realized I had seriously fucked up, but the experience had stirred up so many things inside me I didn't know what to do. How did I explain to him that kissing him aroused me more than anything ever had before? How could I admit I was dying for another taste of his passion? How did I confess dancing with him like that made me want to throw him down on the bed and kiss him senseless before fucking his perfect arse? That I had been feeling this way for almost three years?

"You didn't have to take it that far!" he exclaimed in a hurt voice. "What were you thinking?"

"It felt right."

He wrinkled his brow at my answer. "What the fuck does that mean?"

"I saw the girls kissing and—"

"And you thought you'd make out with me to impress them? What the actual fuck, Ambrose? That's taking a joke too far, even for you."

My gaze drifted down to his lips, once again filling

me with the urge to kiss him again. I refocused my attention. "It wasn't a joke."

"What, so you're saying you kissed me for real?"

"Yes." I closed the distance between us until I was in his personal space once more. I tilted his chin, running my thumb over his plump lower lip. This was my last chance to tell him the truth before I possibly lost him forever. It was now or never. "And I liked it."

An interesting noise escaped him at my confession, but he didn't move away. It gave me the confidence to act. I captured his lips in another kiss. Without the pulse-pounding music driving my actions, it was more intimate, but still deeply enjoyable. My pleasure was short-lived because he jerked back with a swear.

The sound of his anguish pained my heart. "Stop it! There's no one here to pretend for, so quit acting like you're my boyfriend!"

"That's not what I'm doing," I insisted.

"You have no right to fuck with me like this!"

It bothered me that was what he thought I was doing to him. For every step I took toward him, he moved away, until I had him pinned against the wall. Pressed against him again, the desire for him I had on the dance floor returned with a vengeance. "I'm not fucking with you, Augie. I would never do that to you!"

"You got caught up in the heat of the moment," he said. "Stop acting like any of this was real."

It was an easy out, but it wasn't what I wanted. "It was real to me."

"No, it doesn't matter when you're straight."

The comment confused me. "But you're straight, too."

He couldn't meet my gaze. "Wrong."

"You have almost as many ex-girlfriends as I do," I argued. In the entirety of our friendship, I had never once heard Augie express any interest in a man. I almost couldn't wrap my mind around it, if it weren't for the fact I had suspected for a while he might like me that way.

"I also have a bunch of ex-boyfriends you don't know anything about."

The news filled me with conflicting feelings. It hurt that he would hide that from me. I burned with an ugly jealousy at the prospect of another man being with Augie. But it also gave me hope that I stood a real chance with him—provided I hadn't fucked it up by acting impulsively. I focused on the more pressing issue. "You're bisexual?"

"Surprise."

"Why wouldn't you tell me?" We had never kept any secrets from each other before, let alone one this big.

Augie dodged my question with one of his own. "What difference does it make?"

"It matters!"

That finally got him to look up at me. The pain in

his eyes took my breath away as he retorted, "It only matters if you want to be with me. And since you don't—"

When he tried to free himself, I used my larger body to trap him. "You're wrong."

"I'm not. You're straight and not interested in me the same way. Move."

I refused to obey. "My hard-on says otherwise."

"So what?"

My arousal made it a struggle to put my thoughts into words. "I wasn't faking that. I enjoyed kissing you, touching you, and—"

"You were—"

I talked over him to finish my sentence. "I want to do it again."

He shook his head. "You don't mean that."

"I do!"

"No, you don't!" he shot back. "You won't want anything that comes after the kissing. Quit deluding yourself."

When he pushed at my chest to drive me back, I kissed him with the full force of my pent-up lust. He strained against my hold, nipping at my tongue when I tried to delve deeper. It only turned me on more.

Augie was breathless as he warned, "You don't want this."

I pressed my renewed erection against him, letting him feel exactly how wrong he was. "I fucking want you, Augie!"

He taunted me. "Do you really? Are you that desperate to suck my dick? To swallow my cum? Are you prepared to take it up the ass? Because that's where this leads, Ambrose. If you aren't willing to do that or fall in love with me, then stop playing this game with my heart right now."

His words stunned me, allowing him to slip free and escape to the bathroom. He slammed and locked the door behind him. I winced at the noise, still reeling from the encounter.

How did he not understand how much I desperately wanted him? If pressing my raging erection again him while we made out with a fierce desire didn't show him I was serious, what else could I do? How was I supposed to prove to him that the love I felt for him was genuine?

There was a part of me that wanted to break down the bathroom door and demonstrate in explicitly sexual detail how I yearned for him to be mine. However, I forced myself to sit on my bed and take a deep breath. Instead of acting rashly again, I took the time to compose myself and find the right words to convince him about how serious I was. He needed to understand that I wasn't after a meaningless fling to satisfy my sexual curiosity. I wouldn't be satisfied with anything less than his whole heart.

Chapter Five

AUGIE

SAFE IN THE BATHROOM, I berated myself for being so stupid. Ambrose had finally offered me the chance to get what I wanted after years of pining away for him, but I had no choice but to turn him down. It didn't matter that those kisses had been the best of my entire life, or that I had incontrovertible evidence that I aroused him. None of that mattered when he would go back to women after satiating his curiosity with me. It would shatter my broken heart into dust.

I regretted being so cruel in taunting him about being unwilling to accept what being with me would entail. Hurt as I may have been, I had no right to lash out at him like that. Maybe he would have been willing to do those kinds of things if I had eased him into it, but I had ruined any chance of that now.

It was too difficult to think with my mind clouded

by angry arousal. Despite Ambrose being on the other side of the door, I got into the shower to give myself some relief. I was still hard as a rock, tortured by what could have been. In true masochistic fashion, I used some of his body wash to help get me off to the smell of him as I stroked my hardness.

Surrounded by his scent, I sagged against the cold tile wall as I roughly jerked off. At first, I replayed memories of kissing him in the club as we rutted against each other. It quickly morphed into a fantasy of what might have happened if I had let him ravage me in the hotel room like he had clearly wanted to.

"You don't want this."

Ambrose looked down at me with a fire in his eyes as he insisted, "I fucking want you, Augie!"

"Then prove it."

"With pleasure." That was all he said before capturing my lips in a searing kiss as he pressed me back against the wall, letting me feel his impressive arousal.

My fingers entwined in his auburn hair, helping me hold on as our passionate desire for each other grew more desperate. It was what I wanted, but my need to be contrarian drove me to ask, "All you want to do is kiss me?"

"So impatient."

My indignation flared. "You don't get to call me impatient when I've been waiting eight years for this."

He slid his hand down my briefs, cupping my erection and refocusing my attention. I melted further when he promised in a silken voice, "I'm about to make it up to you, darlin'." He started by stripping us both of our clothes before he picked me up and carried me the short distance to the bed.

True to his word, Ambrose set about kissing and touching every inch of me. I basked in his erotic worship of me, but I didn't have the patience for that kind of treatment at the moment. "Make love to me later. Fuck me now."

His chuckle sent a shiver down my spine. "As you wish."

My body arched up under his touch as he finally became serious. There was no trace of gentleness as he gave me the aggressive, dominating fuck I desired, making me cry out his name with wild abandon. I got off on being pinned down by his strength as he took me hard. Driven to my edge, I touched myself in search of the ultimate pleasure as he pushed me to my limits with every thrust of his hips.

"Let me hear that beautiful voice of yours as you come," he purred, his blue eyes dark with a burning lust that set my soul on fire.

I obliged him in the privacy of my mind, but I bit my lower lip in real life to smother my moan as I came in my hand. It gave me a physical release, but I didn't feel any better for it. If anything, I felt awful for getting off on something Ambrose would find abhorrent. It was one thing for him to kiss me, but he would never get on his knees for me and suck my dick or want to fuck me. The thought of it would disgust him. I was a terrible friend for fantasizing about him, knowing being with me like that would repulse and horrify him.

It was even worse now that he knew I was bisexual. When we met as freshmen in college, he had made enough "jokes" about gay men for me to keep that side of my romantic history a secret. As we grew closer, I questioned if his bluster stemmed from a place of fear about himself, but I was never brave enough to bring it up with him. He stopped being offensive as we got older, but there was a part of me that still feared I'd lose him if he found out the truth.

Hiding my sexuality had been easy to do considering I had quit hooking up with men years ago. I used to sleep with guys who had a similar physique or accent, but the copycat experience depressed me too much. There was no substitution for Ambrose, so it was easier to stick to dating women. Even that had become too painful to bear after a point.

My heart clenched in my chest, knowing he most likely had already left the room by now in pursuit of a woman to assert his straightness. The rejection stung, but not nearly as much as the fear that I might have lost my best friend over this whole mess. My inner coward wanted to sweep all of this under the rug and pretend that it was all a joke. Sadly, there wasn't a rug big enough to hide the fact that Ambrose had aroused me tonight. He would know that forever, and it was up to him how he would deal with it. The most I could hope for was that he would act like nothing had happened. I could only pray that he wouldn't renounce our friendship over it.

With a sigh, I shut off the water and got out of

the shower. I would have to face the empty room soon enough, so there was no point in putting it off any longer. For a fleeting moment, I considered using an app to find a man to fuck me into oblivion tonight, but it was pointless. If it wasn't Ambrose, it wasn't worth it.

I HAD BEEN SO convinced Ambrose wouldn't be there when I returned to the room that I exited the bathroom wearing only a towel around my waist. The sight of him sitting on his bed looking at me with a dark hunger in his blue eyes stopped me in my tracks. I immediately regretted my decision while simultaneously celebrating he was still there. He hadn't abandoned me after all. But what the fuck did that mean?

Our impromptu staring contest ended when he stood up and walked over to me. I could barely breathe as he stood close and gazed down at me with genuine desire. For once in my life, I had the good sense not to say a damn word and ruin everything.

He reached out and cupped my face in his large hands, his gaze never leaving mine. His voice was soft as he told me, "I wanted to pretend to be your boyfriend because I feared I'd never have a chance for real. I swear I wasn't doing it to fuck with your feelings, Augie. I'm sorry I was too much of a coward to admit what I really wanted. One night of make-believe was the best I thought I could do."

Was he serious? I stared at him in stunned disbelief. "What?"

"I denied my feelings for a long time because I didn't understand them. But I don't want to run away from you anymore. I want to kiss you again. I want to explore every centimeter of you as I make you moan and claim you as mine. This isn't about only one night or a quick fling. I want all of you forever, Augie."

They were words I had hoped to hear but never thought he would utter, let alone mean. The pessimist in me feared it was too good to be true and needed reassurance. "Only me?"

"There's no one else I have ever wanted more than you." He brushed his thumbs against my cheeks with so much gentleness that it almost broke me. "I want you and only you. You never have to doubt that."

My stupid mouth said before I could stop it, "But I'm not a woman."

"No, you most definitely are not." His lips quirked into a grin. "You're you, and that's the thing I love about you most of all."

He leaned in slowly, giving me the opportunity to reject him if I wanted to. When I didn't pull back, he kissed me with a devastating sweetness that melted my heart. The affection conveyed almost brought tears to my eyes at its perfection. As often as I had longed for fiery make-out sessions with Ambrose, that tenderness was what I yearned for more than anything else.

"If you can be patient with me, I'm willing to learn," he promised. "After all, if Lucien and Rhys can figure this out, we can, too."

I could have laughed at his competitive streak kicking in, but I didn't. "Do you honestly think you could learn to love me?"

His broad hands slid down the curve of my spine, sending shivers through me. "I learned that lesson a long time ago. Let me show you how much."

How could I say no?

Chapter Six

I GUIDED Augie closer to the bed, but he stopped short of it with a frown. He asked, "But what about Katie? And what's-her-name from the strip club?"

It was a fair question. "Nothing happened with either of them. Katie begged for another chance to be with me, but I told her no. I lied about meeting up with the stripper."

"Then where the hell have you been the last two nights?"

"By myself in a room on the eighth floor."

He looked even more baffled by my answer. "Why would you stay there and not in our room?"

It was embarrassing to admit, but I was done hiding the truth from him. "Because I didn't trust myself to be alone with you in this room and not permanently fuck up our friendship."

Augie rubbed his forehead as he attempted to

piece everything together. "What are you talking about?"

"The morning after your birthday last month proved to me that I couldn't be trusted to be alone with you."

He rolled his eyes at my concern. "Oh, please. Do you seriously think our eight years of friendship would be destroyed by accidental morning wood?"

"It wasn't an accident." I pulled him closer until our bodies were flush against each other. The very nearness of him aroused me all over again. "Waking up with you in my arms was like a dream. I knew it was wrong, but holding you as I fantasized about all the sexy ways I wished I could say good morning to you was an incredible turn-on. When you rocked against me, I almost lost it. I left because I was scared you'd wake up and find out."

"And to jerk off," he added with a smirk. "Because that's what I did after you went to hide in the bathroom."

The thought of him getting off on waking up in my arms flooded me with renewed desire. "In my defense, I didn't want to ruin your birthday."

"Ruin my birthday?" He laughed at the notion. "That was one of the best damn parts of it, minus the fact you left. I was ready to roll over and do something about your situation, but I assumed it would have disgusted you to know how much being held by you aroused me. That's why I pretended to still be asleep."

Hearing that Augie had suffered with the same dilemma I had both comforted me and made me feel like the world's biggest idiot. "I consoled myself with knowing nothing could have happened even under the best of circumstances with your dad and Felix in the house. But being alone together in this hotel room, the temptation to give in to my urges to be with you was too risky."

He pinched the bridge of his nose with a long-suffering sigh. "Okay, so let me get this straight. You've spent the last two nights alone in a separate hotel room because you wanted to be with me, while I've spent the past two nights alone here wishing you wanted to be with me. Do I have that right? Because if I do, we're fucking idiots."

"It sure looks that way." I laughed, because otherwise it was too depressing. "Even now, I don't think you fully appreciate how much willpower it's taking me to not strip that towel off of you and commit every centimeter of you to memory."

His cheeks turned a cute shade of pink. "R-really?"

"Being this close to you and not be able to touch you is the worst kind of hell." It was an understatement of epic proportions.

"Do you honestly want me like that?" His nervousness once again made itself known. "It doesn't gross you out?"

I could be delicate about the matter, but that

wasn't my style. "Trust me, I've fantasized about sucking your cock so often that I'll be very disappointed if I'm not an instant expert at it."

His blush turned flame red. "Whoa, okay, um…"

Bashful Augie was always a joy to play with. "I don't remember the last time I fell asleep where making love to you wasn't the final thought on my mind."

"That's almost romantic in a dumbass kind of way," he said, a hint of a smile on his face.

"I could graphically describe all the various ways I've imagined us being together, but I'd rather show you."

His hands trembled as he helped me strip off my black tank. "Fine, but I refuse to be the only one naked for this." I tossed it onto the floor, causing him to inhale sharply as he studied my muscles. "Good god, and you think you need to hit the gym more often?"

"No, but it's the best place for me to work off my repressed sexual frustration. Maybe now you'll understand how long I've been fighting my attraction for you."

His fingertips glided over my impressive abs, causing them to clench. He continued studying my muscular chest, not quite able to meet my gaze. "But you never said anything."

I snorted at that. "It's not my fault you thought me talking about waking up married to you and having sex was subtle. Not only did I say I would try it, but I asked you if you'd be fine with it to make sure it was okay. Hell, I suggested we hook up together with the girls and see where the night would take us, while volunteering to be your boyfriend. How much more obvious did I have to be that I was dying to be with you if only you'd let me?"

"*That's* what you were trying to do?"

"Why else did you think I started hitting on hot guys in front of you all the time recently?"

"Because you're an unrepentant flirt who will banter with anyone remotely attractive?" he guessed.

He had a point about that, but there was more to it than that. "It was my way of showing you I was open to being with a guy as long as it was you."

Augie laughed so hard he doubled over and held on to me for support. He wiped tears of mirth away from his eyes. "God, we're so damn dumb. We can never make fun of Rhys and Lucien for being dense about their feelings for each other ever again."

"Agreed." As amusing as this was, I was interested in moving on, so I stripped off my jeans to redirect his attention to more pressing matters. I tugged on the band of my black briefs. "Shall I do the honors, or do you want to?"

He took his time sliding them off, copping a feel of my arse in the process. My prominent erection sprung free, a testament to how aroused being with Augie made me. It begged for attention, but I would be satisfied with anything he was willing to give me, even if it was nothing at all.

"May I?" I asked, gesturing at his towel.

He nodded his consent, so I wasted no time in pulling it from his waist to drop to the floor. His body was a thing of great beauty to me. I loved his softness that contrasted my hard muscles. Forever wouldn't be long enough to treasure him, but I would give it my best effort.

I guided him to lie back on the bed, caging him in place with my larger frame. It hardly seemed real that he was finally under me and willing, but I set about exploring his body with kisses and touches. His responsiveness drove me wild with lust, but I stayed focused.

As I neared his prick, I smelled a hint of my body wash on him. That he had used it to get himself off after our fight excited me on a primal level. "Oh, you're a naughty lad, aren't you?"

Lulled into complacency by my gentle attention, he could only hum, "Hmm?"

"I fucking love it." My ego preened over what he had done. I rewarded him by running my tongue along the underside of his erection. The taste of my teakwood body wash was faint but unmistakable. "You have my permission to do that again whenever you want."

"What are you—*oh!*"

I wasn't sure if his exclamation was about realizing I knew what he had done or a reaction to my actions, but I wanted him to do it again. "How do you always find new ways to drive me wild?"

Without giving him an opportunity to answer, I decided it was now or never. I wrapped my lips around the head of his cock and slid it into my mouth. His shocked gasp was delicious. I got him nice and wet before taking him deeper while working the base with my hand. His fingers scrambled for purchase in my hair as I continued making him come undone by bobbing along his length while I sucked him off.

"Ambro—*oh, god*! Fuck!"

His breathy swears and moans deeply gratified me. It may have been my first time giving a blow job for real, but I had done my due diligence by practicing on a dildo. This was a million times better than working unyielding silicone. I groaned in satisfaction around him, resisting the urge to jerk myself off simultaneously like I normally did when I was alone.

He whimpered my name in fractured syllables, trying to push me back as he warned, "Stop, I'm too close."

There was nothing that would keep me from enjoying that. Instead of backing off, I relaxed my throat and took him as deep as I could. I gagged a little, which triggered his orgasm. I swallowed his release, quite pleased with myself and my performance. The picture of him looking ravished and satiated was one that would stay in my memory forever.

He struggled to form words. "Why the hell are you so good at that?"

"I took precautions to ensure that if I was ever blessed enough to be with you that I would know how to satisfy you."

His brow wrinkled in confusion. "Reading a 'Ten Tips to Make Your Guy Lose His Mind When He Comes' blog article doesn't get those kinds of results." I laughed, but he still looked disturbed. "Why did that feel like your hundredth time giving oral and not your first?"

"You honor me, sir. If you must know, I practiced."

A shadow passed over his gorgeous green eyes. "Please tell me you mean on a banana and not random men."

"Augusto has been very obliging."

"*Augusto?*"

"Yes, he's been very accommodating to my increasingly frequent practices of late," I teased. "Then again, I suppose it's hard to complain when you're a dildo."

Augie shoved my shoulder with a grumble. "You dick, I thought you meant a real person!"

"The only cock I have any interest in pleasuring is yours," I promised him. "I'm so happy to know my time with Augusto was well spent."

"Did you use it to practice anything else?"

"Are you asking me if Augusto has been up my arse?" The flush on Augie's face confirmed I was right. "I must say, I'm enjoying your jealous streak over me."

He tried to defend himself. "I never thought you'd be okay with that."

With a smirk, I put on a show of stroking my hardness, smearing the bead of precum that had gathered. "Trust me, I'm *very* much looking forward to that practice paying off with you later."

He covered his face with a groan. "You're killing me. You know that, right?"

"The person who has gotten off twice tonight while I'm still suffering with the hard-on from hell is in no position to say that."

"Hey, you should've considered that before wearing me the fuck out," he retorted, making us laugh. "Fine, get up here."

"What do you mean?"

The challenging look in his eyes made my erection twitch with interest. "I mean get up here and fuck my mouth while I show you how it's done."

"Holy hell, Augie."

"I'll send you to heaven soon." He gestured for me to come closer. "Don't hold back, because I'm not stopping until you've finished."

After some careful repositioning, I knelt over Augie, who immediately took me so deep that his nose touched my trimmed pubes. Taking him at his word, I held onto the headboard for balance as I lightly thrusted in and out of his mouth. He deep-throated me as I moved with increasing confidence once I realized I wasn't hurting him. It amazed me that absolutely nothing triggered his gag reflex. The way he groped my arse and used it to pull me in deeper was almost more than I could handle. I tightened my grip on the wooden frame, which creaked in protest under the strain.

His finger circling my hole with the slightest tease of penetration, combined with humming around my prick, was too intense. I cried out Augie's name as I emptied into his throat with the most satisfying orgasm of my life. Good lord, he wasn't kidding about putting me to shame. I trembled from the overwhelming intensity of my release. It took an effort to move back. When I did, he pulled me down for a kiss that was tender compared to what I had just done to his mouth. His lips were slick and swollen, which would have aroused me again if I was physically capable of it. Everything about him drove me wild.

I settled down next to Augie, lying on my side so I could look at him. The experience gave me the courage to admit, "Just so you know, you were jealous of yourself earlier."

His eyebrows furrowed as he stared at me with a confused expression. "What are you talking about?"

"Who I took to the cabin," I clarified, referring to

the story I had told at the restaurant. It had been the first thing he had asked me about after we returned to our room. "I was telling the truth that I never went there with anyone. It was a fantasy I often have about us going together."

"Seriously?" I couldn't blame him for looking so skeptical. Even I found it hard to believe sometimes. "You're joking, right?"

"Nope, it's the god's honest truth. It was one of the many destinations I imagined us escaping to for a romantic weekend together."

He hid his face as he laughed against the sheets. "I thought I was the only one who did that."

"Beach daydreams are nice, minus the reality that sand gets *everywhere* and is not at all sexy or pleasant."

Augie snorted in amusement. "Yeah, I learned the hard way that sex and sand are a terrible combination." He flushed beautifully. "Sometimes I'd imagine what it would be like to go to Dublin with you."

"Same. I'd love to make that happen someday."

"That would be amazing."

He was too cute for words. I reached over and pulled him into a hug, my heart full of love for my best friend. I placed a gentle kiss on his forehead. "I'll go anywhere in the world, so long as it's together with you." Augie nuzzled against me with a happy noise. "What do you say we start with a trip to the shower?"

His beautiful smile made me fall in love with him all over again. "I like the sounds of that."

Although I could have gladly remained in bed with him forever, I got out and held my hand out to him to help him out of it. I interlaced our fingers as we headed to the bathroom, where I intended to enjoy him being wet and naked in the shower. It was like the best kind of dream, except it was even better because it was real.

WHEN I AWOKE in the morning, I was curled up around Augie, clutching him like my favorite teddy bear. My mind still fuzzy with sleep, I was in no rush to hurry and wake up yet. Instead, I enjoyed holding him from behind, loving the way he fit perfectly against my body as if he was made for me. We were like two puzzle pieces that came together to make a whole. I could hardly believe he wanted me as much as I wanted him. How I had gotten so lucky was beyond me.

Once again, it reminded me of the day after his last birthday. I had woken up in the same position spooning him, his perfect arse pressed against my hardness and giving me ideas I wasn't brave enough to try.

This time was different, though. Now, I knew for a fact that he reciprocated my feelings. As he shifted in his sleep, my prick perked up with interest. I grew bolder as I trailed my fingers down the length of his body. He rocked against me with a breathy moan but didn't wake up.

I grinned when I encountered his erection, loving that he instinctively moaned my name. His reaction overjoyed me, because it proved that even asleep, he wanted me. Despite last night, part of me still found it almost impossible to believe that we were finally on the same page about how we felt for each other. I kept my touch light and teasing, relishing the privilege of being allowed to do so.

He groaned, so I stilled from further explorations. To my great surprise and delight, he grumbled, "Damn it, don't just fucking stop."

Chuckling at the reaction, I obliged him by gripping his hot and heavy length. My voice was rough with sleep when I asked, "Is this what you want?"

"*Yes!*" His hips bucked against me, amusing me with his impatience. "More!"

Entertained by his reaction, I picked up speed as I jerked him off while trailing kisses along his bare shoulder. I rocked my hard length against his arse, moaning next to his ear as I got off on pleasuring him. My only regret was that I couldn't see his lovely face in that position.

As if sensing my thoughts, Augie rolled over and pushed me onto my back to straddle me. I savored the image of him over me, the sight of his flushed cheeks and prominent arousal begging me to continue. When he moaned, "Please, Ambrose," with need, there was no holding back.

I resumed trying to get him off but faltered when he rubbed my cock along the crease of his ass. He thrust against it without penetration. It was equal parts enjoyable and distracting, but I did my best to stay focused on my primary goal of pleasuring Augie.

"So close," he whimpered. True to his word, it only took a few more strokes before he exploded all over my fist with a gasp. It was such a deeply erotic sight that it drew out my orgasm as well.

Augie was the first to move as he leaned forward and claimed my lips for his own. As he teased me with his tongue, I brought him down with my clean hand for a deeper taste.

After we parted, he greeted me, "Good morning."

"It sure is."

He laughed and melted against me, bonelessly sprawled on top of me. I held him closer, uncaring of the mess between us. In that moment, I had everything I wanted right there in my arms. The world could wait a little longer.

Chapter Seven

AUGIE

AMBROSE HAD INSISTED on taking me on a proper date before we did anything more than last night. He had been a charming gentleman throughout, romancing me in a way I never thought possible. Everything had been so perfect that I half expected to wake up and discover the whole thing was a dream.

After we finished dinner, I asked him about what had been bugging me the most. "What changed for this to be okay for you?"

"I was finally honest with myself. You have to remember, I grew up in a very conservative Irish Catholic family. They raised me to believe being gay was a sin that would lead to an eternal life of damnation."

While I didn't wish to make light of his situation, I pointed out, "So does having premarital sex. That certainly never stopped you."

He chuckled. "Aye, that's true. I walked away from the Church's doctrines when I left home, so I set about to have a grand time to compensate for denying myself earlier. But certain things were easier to cast off than others."

"Meaning?"

"Having a girlfriend wouldn't bother anybody," he explained. "But if I had a boyfriend, I probably wouldn't have a home to return to."

The thought made my stomach twist into knots. After Mom died, my brother, Dad, and I became even more close-knit. Family was everything to me because I knew how quickly life could tear it from you in an instant. "I'm sorry."

Ambrose waved away my apology. "Don't be. Being happy is worth testing the limits of their Christian forgiveness."

"But if they don't approve—"

"Then that's their problem. I'm done running from what I want." He picked up my hand and held it in his, brushing his thumb over my knuckles. "I need you more than their approval."

The declaration was sweet, but the possibility of Ambrose losing everything because of being with me made me ill. "But they're your family."

"Yes, but I love you."

He stated it so easily, sending a million butterflies aflutter within me. I still found it difficult to understand. "How? You've never liked guys before."

"I wouldn't say 'never,' but it's true I've never been serious about one until you," he said. "Growing up, I always explained away those stray thoughts about finding a guy arousing. I learned how to ignore that part of myself. But eventually, I had to accept the depths of my feelings for you."

"When?"

"After Rhys's last pool party."

The answer stunned me. "But that was almost three years ago!" I wracked my brain trying to recall what happened but drew a blank. "Did I do something?"

Ambrose rotated his empty glass before saying, "In a manner of speaking."

I couldn't remember anything I might have done that would have changed things between us. "What does that mean?"

"It means I saw something I shouldn't have." He paused before continuing. "I was looking for you when I caught you hooking up with that redhead."

The information still didn't ring any bells for me. There had been countless women over the years, so they all blurred together. "I don't remember that at all."

"You couldn't see me." Ambrose's blue eyes focused on me with an intensity that set my soul ablaze. "But I saw you. She had you pinned against the wall as you made out, before she went down on you."

His words recalled the memory. I had been so sexually frustrated and angry at seeing Ambrose in his nearly nude glory and having all the gorgeous women hanging all over him. Under normal circumstances, I never would have been bold enough to get a blow job from a random girl in Rhys's house. However, when the redhead offered herself, I had jumped at the chance for some relief. My logic was anything had to be better than watching all those girls touching him in ways I could only fantasize about. "*Oh.*"

He continued his story. "Even though it was wrong, it was so hot seeing you get off with her. I almost lost it when you orgasmed."

The knowledge that he had been that aroused because of me getting sucked off by some girl was sexy as hell. "Wow, I had no idea."

"I immediately locked myself in the nearest bathroom to take care of myself. I came so hard I practically saw stars, but I didn't question it then."

"But later?"

"Whenever I got off after that, even if I started by fantasizing about a woman, that memory of you coming kept popping into my mind. I refused to acknowledge why I was so fixated on you and your pleasure. It wasn't until I accidentally inserted myself into the fantasy to be with you that I realized what was happening."

"What did you do?"

He grinned. "Stayed in denial about it for a long

time. But I grew more comfortable with my desire for you when I thought maybe you felt the same way about me. That's why it confused me when any attempts at flirting with you pissed you off instead."

The stupidity of it caused me to groan. "It drove me nuts because you kept tempting me with what I wanted most and could never have!"

Ambrose at least had the decency to look sheepish about it. "Sorry about that."

"I'm sure you can make it up to me."

The devilish twinkle in his eyes sent a thrill through me. "Oh, I've got a few ideas."

BACK IN OUR HOTEL ROOM, we fumbled off our clothes as soon as the door shut. It was a race for who could get naked first in between hungry kisses. I loved how Ambrose claimed my mouth, dominating my desires as he backed us closer to the bed. It sent all my blood rushing south.

"Tell me what you want, Augie."

My hands roamed up his washboard abs and over his chest to wrap around his neck in a loose hold. "I want you." Talk about massive understatements.

"Maybe how do you want it is a better question." He fondled my ass, making it impossible to reply. "Should I make love to you and show you how I feel? Would you rather a rough fuck to release all our pent-up desires? Or, would you like to take me——"

Everything sounded perfect. "Yes, to all of it."

"Will you give yourself to me tonight?"

I pulled him down for another hungry kiss. "Tonight, and every other night."

Ambrose picked me up like I weighed nothing and laid me down on the bed. He covered me with his massive body, careful not to crush me under his weight as he pressed close to claim my lips once more. The tenderness melted my heart as he worshipped me in awe, kissing and touching me everywhere all at once. It didn't feel fair I got to lie back and enjoy it, especially when I wished to do the same to him. There was time for that later, though.

Before I could plead for respite, he slid a slicked finger into me. I wasn't sure where he had magically procured lube from, but I welcomed the progress. He combined it with lavishing each of my balls with attention. For someone who hadn't been with a man before, he was shockingly skilled at it.

When it was too much to bear, I begged, "Please, I'm good." I bit back a groan at the sudden emptiness when he withdrew. That disappointment morphed into anticipation when he put on a condom before lining himself up to penetrate me.

Ambrose slowly slid into me. The consideration was nice, considering how long it had been since I had bottomed. To finally have the one man inside me I had been dreaming about for years was the best kind of heaven.

"Fucking hell, you're tight." He trembled from the effort it took not to move yet. I gave in to my urge to play with him a little by clenching around his hard length. "Fuck!"

"Whenever you're ready to." I rocked my hips in silent permission.

He kissed me with a passion that stole my breath away before he moved in earnest. I held onto his broad shoulders, enjoying the flex of his muscles under my fingertips. He made tender love to me, murmuring sweet things in that sexy accent of his as his touch further heightened my pleasure. It was so gratifying to have everything I desired after so many years of longing that it almost brought me to tears.

"You're so beautiful." He looked down at me as if I was the most precious thing in the entire world to him. "I love you, Augie."

Normally, I would have worried about how fast things were moving. However, after almost a decade of being in love with Ambrose, it was a relief to admit it out loud. "I love you, too." There weren't enough words for how much, so I let my body tell him the truth.

Chapter Eight

IF I HAD KNOWN it would feel this good to give in to my feelings for Augie, I wouldn't have resisted for so many years. There was nothing better than being intimately embraced by him as we moved as one.

As much as I looked forward to a passionate fuck, making love to him was incredible. I had always enjoyed sex with women, but none of my hookups could hold a candle to the emotional connection I shared with Augie. It made everything more intense and special. I had never felt as close to someone as I did to him. Truly, I had been an idiot to run away from him for so long.

His body yielded to mine, welcoming me with each roll of my hips. He held on to me, surrendering to me in a way that I would never take for granted. Augie awash in pleasure was the most beautiful thing

I had ever seen. The moment seared into my mind to remember always.

He tensed as he neared his peak. It wouldn't be long for either of us, so I worked his hardness to drive him over the edge. He keened as he thrusted into my fist, throwing off our rhythm. It only took a few strokes before his whole body arched and he came, crying out my name. His cum spurted onto his stomach, which was an unexpected turn-on for me.

With a few more thrusts, I moaned as I climaxed with a shudder. I leaned down and captured his lips in a sweet kiss, overwhelmed by my love for him. Any doubts I may have still had over whether this was the right thing for me and our friendship disappeared without a trace. I had a new clarity about how much I needed this beautiful man in my life. Even though being with a guy was uncharted territory for me, I wanted to embrace him with my whole heart that belonged to him and him alone.

After pulling out of him, I tied off and cast aside the used condom. When I lay down next to August, he shifted positions so he could curl up and rest his head on my shoulder. I wrapped an arm around him, cradling him against me. Having him nestled in my embrace brought a sense of peace and rightness unlike anything I had experienced before, but found I very much enjoyed.

WE EVENTUALLY CLEANED up before getting back in bed together to cuddle. I wished we could stay in Las Vegas longer. The morning would come too soon, and we would fly back home to Sunnyside. I had no reason to be apprehensive about it, but I required answers about what would change.

That was why I asked Augie, "Can we talk about what changes once we're home?"

He tensed against me. "Sure."

I traced invisible patterns on his bare shoulder to soothe us both. "This isn't a 'what happens in Vegas, stays in Vegas' situation for me."

Augie relaxed against me with a relieved sigh. "Oh, thank god."

His reaction surprised me. "Did you think I would insist we go back to normal once we returned?"

He hesitated before saying, "I don't know. If you regretted it and thought you made a huge mistake, maybe you would prefer to act like none of this ever happened."

I guided him to sit up. He did a terrible job of hiding his fear from me. I caressed his cheek as I reassured him. "My only regrets are not being honest with you about this earlier and wasting years being in denial about what I feel for you. Telling you the truth and being with you is the best decision of my life, not my biggest mistake. I have no doubts about that."

Worry still clung to him. "But what about your family? They—"

"They're an ocean away and have nothing to do with this. I'll deal with them later." I cut his next protest off with a kiss. "It is what it is. I meant what I said before. I want you more than their approval."

Augie persisted. "Would you really be okay if Callum hates you because of me?"

"I won't lie. I'd be absolutely gutted if my younger brother shunned me for loving you. The loss would be hard, but living without you would be even worse."

He looked down, unable to hold my gaze any longer. "You're so close to him, though. He worships you."

"Cally is also younger and more open-minded," I explained, using his family nickname. "It may take him a little while to get over the initial shock, but I don't think he'll write me off forever. I trust that our bond is deeper than that."

"I would feel so guilty if he turned against you because of me. Not to mention your parents."

His concern about my family wasn't surprising, given how close he was with his father and brother after losing his mom. "Augie, look at me." I waited until he complied to continue. "I've decided to be happy with you no matter what anyone thinks. If my folks shun me, then that's the price I'm willing to pay."

"You shouldn't have to!"

"I'll cross that bridge when it's time. I've made my choice to be with you, and nothing will change my mind." I tried to guide the conversation back on track. "That's why we need to discuss what happens next."

"What do you want to happen?"

I told him the truth. "I want to be your boyfriend, and go on dates, and be with you."

A smile finally graced his face as he looked up at me. "You seriously want to be my boyfriend?"

"Nothing would make me happier."

"You don't do the dating thing, though," he said. "You were with women all the time, but you never stayed with any of them long enough to get serious."

There was no defense to that claim since it was true, but it didn't mean I wouldn't tease him about it. "Hey, I didn't say I'd be any good at it. But I'll try for you."

His laughter chased away the last of his doubt. "Well, look on the bright side. You've already met my dad and Felix. They both like you, so that's half the battle right there."

"Do you think this will come as a surprise to them?"

He rolled his eyes at the question. "Did you forget my brother recommending you tie me up in bed to keep me from rushing home to his defense? He's known for years."

The reminder made me chuckle. "Ah, that explains that weirdly specific suggestion. One I'm not opposed to if you're into that kind of thing."

"I'm not saying no to later, but next time, I want my hands free when I get my turn to explore you."

My prick perked up at that, but I ignored it. "I look forward to it."

"Unfortunately, it'll have to wait until tomorrow. It's late, and our flight is too damn early in the morning. I agreed to help Felix move out of Danny's apartment after we land."

Translation: no more sex today. That was fine, since snuggling with Augie was its own form of pleasure. "I can also assist if he wants."

"Good, because I already volunteered you," he said with a laugh. I loved that he always relied on me. "Just be prepared for Felix to make a million smart-ass comments about us finally getting together."

"I'd expect nothing less from him." Felix reminded me of Callum, so I enjoyed spending time with him. "Come on, let's get some sleep."

I shut off the lights before we settled into bed. Spooning Augie from behind satisfied me to the core of my soul as I held him close.

Chapter Nine

AUGIE

AFTER FLYING BACK TO SUNNYSIDE, Ambrose and I headed straight over to help Felix move out of Danny's apartment. By late afternoon, we had almost finished packing up the last of my brother's things when we took a break. It had taken real willpower to not get distracted by Ambrose's enormous biceps in his tight green T-shirt every time he carried a heavy box out to the car. Whenever he picked up something with ease, I pictured him doing that to me in the bedroom, but that fantasy would have to wait until later.

Felix dropped into the single seat with a tired sigh. In his faded band shirt and ratty jeans, he looked like a lanky kid instead of a twenty-two-year-old. No matter how old he got, he would always be my baby brother. The family resemblance between us was strong, since we had similar face shapes with prominent cheekbones and delicate eyebrows. We both had green eyes, but mine were a shade of jade, while his were closer to gray.

I had worried about him after his initial phone call two days ago, but he was surprisingly upbeat under the circumstances. "How are you holding up?"

He ran his hand through his hair, spiking it up in a way that made him appear even more boyish. "Better than I was. Wren and Izzy helped give me some perspective on the situation. My new roommate, North, seems like a cool guy which helps. I met his twin sister, West. She's hilarious."

"They're seriously named North and West?"

"Oh, it gets more ridiculous. I assumed he was joking when he said his name was North Easton, but it's honest to god on his driver's license."

I had to laugh at the names. "But if they're twins, shouldn't they be North and South?"

"Their mom wanted them to be closer instead of polar opposites of each other, so she picked West since East Easton is the most ridiculous name of them all. North's mom also has a cat named Woof that she dresses up in costumes and posts pictures of him on social media all the time. They're an interesting bunch."

"It sounds like there won't be many dull moments." Ambrose stretched his arm out behind me, brushing my shoulder with his thumb.

"I'm relieved you found someone to live with so quickly."

Felix looked around the drab living room. "I definitely won't miss this place and its superthin walls that let you hear every time your neighbor farted."

I was pleased to see him keeping things in perspective. "You seem to be handling this pretty well so far."

"Once I got over the initial shock of it, I understood what everyone had been saying. He was a terrible boyfriend."

"And a shitty excuse for a person," Ambrose added. I loved how protective he was of my brother.

"That, too." Felix shrugged. "The problem is, I was so desperate for a boyfriend I let it cloud my judgment and I settled for the first guy who showed any interest in me. I won't make that mistake twice."

"You have plenty of time to be serious about someone later," Ambrose said. "You're the age where you're supposed to have fun and run wild."

Felix curled his legs under him as he made himself more comfortable. "Yeah, but I'm not interested in screwing my way through all the dating apps."

"Thank you for that." It would be hypocritical to tell him not to fuck around, but I didn't want him hurt by assholes.

"I prefer the stability of a real relationship with someone you can come home to every night who will always be there for you," Felix said with another sigh. "It's so much better to be with one person who gets all your stupid in-jokes and loves you, regardless. That means more than a meaningless fuck with a hot guy whose name you won't remember afterward. Nobody my age wants that, though."

"So, date someone older," Ambrose suggested.

I shot him a warning glare. The last thing I wanted was some sugar daddy preying on my brother.

"A silver fox interested in me because I look like barely legal jailbait isn't my thing, either," Felix said as he wrinkled his nose in distaste. "I'm not one to yuck anyone's yum, but the daddy kink doesn't do it for me."

I grimaced at the memory of an encounter I had with that type. Because it was my brother, I spoke without a filter. "I had a guy who told me to call him Daddy once, and I told him to call a therapist to work on his issues. He thought I was trying to entice him to spank me in punishment, which was my cue to get the hell out of there."

The possessive fury in Ambrose's blue eyes thrilled me. His voice came out in a growl that sent shivers through me. "When was this?"

"A period of my life where I made a lot of bad decisions," I retorted, trying to keep the mood light.

It didn't work. He was more insistent as he demanded, "When?"

Felix snickered at his reaction. "I totally guessed you'd be the caveman type."

The genuine upset on Ambrose's handsome face twisted my stomach in knots, making me regret bringing it up. I didn't want to confess, but I knew he would make up a worse story in his mind if I didn't. "When we went to that bonfire party at Ronnie's parents' beach house our freshmen year."

He furrowed his brow in confusion. "But you went home early."

"Right, because after I told his dad no, I refused to stick around," I explained. "At first it was sexy when he came on to me, but when he started in on the daddy stuff, it grossed me out because of Ronnie. People always mistook us for brothers because we looked alike, so being a stand-in for him creeped me out. It was easier to leave."

My answer seemed to upset Ambrose more. "You told me you were sick."

"Freshman year you wouldn't have been ready to hear, 'Hey, I was down to fuck Ronnie's hot dad until he wanted to punish me, so I bailed.' Besides, it wasn't a total lie. It made me sick to my stomach thinking his dad wanted me because I strongly resembled his son." I shuddered in revulsion. "I know that's not the case with every guy who's into the daddy Dom thing—and more power to them for liking what they like. However, Ronnie and I looked too much alike for it to be okay with me."

"I would have fucking killed him if I knew that was why you left." He looked like he still wanted to now.

While sweet, it wasn't true. "If it happened today, I don't doubt that. But the old you would have been too disgusted by me being willing to let him fuck me to do anything other than stop being my friend. I didn't want that, so I left without a word. To this day, Ronnie still doesn't know about the incident. I'm sorry, I shouldn't have brought it up."

My heart sank when Ambrose got up and announced, "I'll be right back," then walked into Felix's bedroom and shut the door.

"Goddamn it, me and my stupid fucking mouth." I doubled over with a groan and hid my face against my knees. "Why do I never learn?"

Felix rubbed my back. "Just give him a minute to process it. He'll be fine."

I was the world's biggest idiot for bringing up the subject. The worst part was there was no one to blame but myself. "I'm such a dumbass."

"In your defense, you claimed it was a period in your life where you made bad choices." That was less than helpful. "He can't hold that against you now. You obviously learned from it."

A miserable noise escaped me. It terrified me I had just done something that would wreck our nascent relationship.

"Go talk to him."

"He doesn't want to talk to me."

"Talk to him anyway." He poked me in the side, making me jerk in surprise. "It's what you would tell me to do if I was in your position."

He was right. "When did you get so smart?"

"I learned from the best big brother ever," he replied with a smile. "Now, quit stalling and go."

It felt like I was marching off to my death, but I made myself confront the consequences. I knocked on the bedroom door before entering.

Ambrose was sitting on the edge of the bed, hiding his face in his hands as he rested his elbows on his knees. For such a big guy, he looked so small that it unnerved me. I wasn't sure where else to start, so I figured an apology was as good a place as any. "I'm sorry." He didn't react at all. "I was stupid and imma-ture back then, and—"

Without looking at me, he interrupted to say, "You were right."

"Huh?"

His voice cracked in his grief. "I hate that you were right."

"What do you mean?" When he didn't answer me, I sat next to him on the bed.

It took him some time before he admitted, "If I had known what had happened in the past, you're absolutely right, I would have stopped being your friend. I hate myself for that."

His confession stunned me, but I was quick to console him. "Things were different then."

"You had to hide so much of who you were because I was an asshole in deep denial." He sounded on the verge of tears. "You made so many sacrifices to be my friend, even though I was the worst. Why would you have wanted to be friends with me at all back then?"

That was an easy answer. "Because I understood there was more to you than making bad jokes about gay guys out of your insecurity. Besides, you grew out of that ignorance pretty quickly. I couldn't hold it against you knowing what you were raised to believe. What matters most is that you changed."

"I came so close to losing you," he whispered in anguish. "It sickens me I would have made that choice."

Trying to get him to look at me, I knelt on the floor in front of him. "You can't beat yourself up over something you might have theoretically done eight years ago. We all did stupid shit at eighteen as fresh-men, as my story proves. But we learned, and we became better people as we moved on. I'm right here, and I'm yours, as long as you want me."

That finally got him to glance up at me. His agony hurt my heart. He reached out and cupped my cheeks in his large hands. "Of course, I want you. Fuck, I want you more than I've wanted anything in my life. But I don't deserve you. Not after what I did to you."

I nuzzled against his palm. "Yes, you do. I'm not holding any of that against you, and you shouldn't either. We've both grown up since then and learned how to make better choices. That's the important thing."

"How can I ever apologize enough for the way I acted in the past?"

"By forgiving yourself." When he continued staring at me like a lost little boy, I kissed him. "By loving me now without fear."

Ambrose pulled me up into a crushing hug. I returned the embrace, allowing me to feel him trembling from the force of his emotional turmoil. I stroked the back of his head in silent comfort. After some time, he said, "Thank you for seeing past all that and loving me anyway."

"I should be the one thanking you for working through all of that and loving me."

He leaned back enough to stare at me with genuine remorse. "I'm sorry it took me so long."

"You were definitely worth the wait." I kissed him again with a little more passion this time.

"I'd be completely lost without you now, Augie. You know that, right?"

"I'm not going anywhere other than home with you tonight."

He smirked at that. "How mad do you think your brother would get if we took advantage of this bed and that closed door as I make it up to you?"

I shifted my balance to push him back onto the bed. "Let's find out."

Ambrose reached down and groped my ass, pulling me closer to him. The thrill of getting caught made it even more arousing. I rutted against him with a soft moan as we kissed.

We froze when there was a knock on the door and my brother called out, "I wanted you two to make up, not make out. I'm starving, so save it for later."

I rested my head on Ambrose's shoulder with a laugh. Felix had cockblocked me on far too many occasions for it to be a surprise.

Ambrose hugged me closer. "But I'm enjoying my snack."

Felix opened the door, snickering when he saw us. "How can you be enjoying your snack if you haven't even unwrapped him yet?"

"I was savoring him."

"Do that on your own time in your own bed. That one's cursed."

"Fine, you've made your point," I sighed, moving off Ambrose.

Satisfied, my brother walked away.

When I followed him, Ambrose caught me by the wrist and pulled me into a bear hug. He kissed the top of my head and whispered, "Thank you."

I enjoyed being held in his strong arms, until my brother yelled out, "Guys!"

Ambrose never could resist teasing my brother. "Is the pizza guy hot or something?"

"Yes, now hurry up!"

With a quick kiss, we left the room hand in hand, relieved that everything was fine.

Chapter Ten

AMBROSE

I NEVER HATED myself more than I did when I realized Augie was right about how the old me would have reacted to finding out he was bisexual. When we'd met our freshman year, I had just arrived in America. It was my first time living away from the Catholic church and my family's influence. The homophobia I had internalized through their religious indoctrination caused me to tell all kinds of awful "jokes" back then that humiliated and disgusted me now. Knowing that every time I had said something hateful, I had unwittingly been hurting my closest friend made me want to crawl in a hole and die. Instead of rightfully telling me to fuck off, he had helped me understand how hurtful those comments were, which was why I had stopped.

When Augie said he understood I had acted that way out of my insecurity, it stuck with me. That was exactly what I had been doing, which he had somehow known all along. He had recognized something in me I hadn't been willing to see and saved me from my own stupidity. I was even more in awe of him because it would have been so easy for him to walk away from me and my bigotry. However, he had stayed and helped me be a better person. Not only that, but he also loved me despite how long it had taken me to come to terms with that part of myself.

Thinking about all the good times I would have missed—especially the bliss of being with him—because of my fear made me sick. It forced me to contend with the fact that by staying so deeply in the closet, I had unintentionally shoved him back into his. The guilt over making him hide parts of himself from me tore me to shreds. He had been right not to trust me, which was the worst part. How could I ever make it up to him?

"You're brooding." Augie's words returned my mind to the present as we sat in my living room after a long day of helping Felix move out of his apartment. "This is about earlier, isn't it?"

"I was an absolute gobshite in the past." The anguish was clear in my voice. "Why didn't you tell me to go fuck myself? After all the awful things I said, why did you stay friends with me?"

"Because I fell in love with you the first day we met and you yelled at a guy, 'Oi, do I look like a *feckin'* leprechaun to you, *eejit*?'" I was impressed and weirdly turned on by how dead-on accurate his imitation of my accent was, but I didn't let myself get distracted. "It was also because you were a scared eighteen-year-old kid living alone in a foreign country and in over your head."

"Only at first. Once we became close friends, it was easier to be apart from my family."

Augie smiled at me. "It was the same for me. I struggled with not being there for Felix and Dad all the time, but you gave me a reason to be okay with it."

"But in the beginning, I said so many awful things about men being together. How could you stand it?"

"I won't lie and say that it didn't hurt, or that I wasn't afraid I would lose you if you found out I also liked guys," he said. "But I knew you grew up Catholic and had been taught gay people were an abomination. I had my suspicions that maybe you weren't as straight as you tried to act and that scared you, so you lashed out."

While it was true, I insisted, "None of that excuses any of it, though."

"No, it doesn't, and the fact that you recognized that gave me hope. Your willingness to open your mind to new perspectives and change for the better is why I put up with the bullshit. Now, you love Felix like your own little brother, even though he's gay. The only time you've ever said a bad thing about his boyfriends was because they broke his heart, not because they were men."

His comment caused me to realize, "It must have terrified you to tell me Felix was gay."

He hesitated. "I was a little nervous, but by then, you liked Felix, so I trusted you. You didn't disappoint me, thank god."

"But you still couldn't tell me about yourself."

Augie took a moment to collect his thoughts. "It was irrelevant by that point. I stopped hooking up with men years ago."

"Why?"

He arched an eyebrow with an expression that silently asked, *Really?*

The reality was a hard punch to the gut. "You were that scared of me finding out?"

"No, it's because none of them were you, and it fucked me up every time." He shrugged as if it wasn't a big deal.

The latter part of his statement confused me. "How so?"

"If they resembled you, it was a painful reminder of what I wanted most and could never have. If they didn't, I fantasized the entire time that it was you instead, which left me hollow afterward. At least with women, the sex was different enough to distract me. But even that quit working after a point." He grinned ruefully. "Now, you know why I was always in a foul mood."

It made my guilt twist in the pit of my stomach. "How could you endure it?"

"A *lot* of masturbation," he joked, trying to lift my spirits. It at least got me to laugh. "How did you?"

"Same." I turned serious once more. "Sometimes, I would catch you looking at me with blatant desire when you thought I was oblivious. You often became flustered whenever I got too close or flirtatious. And not to sound egotistical, but your track record with picking up redheaded Irish gals made me wonder if it was because you secretly wanted me."

He snorted at that. "Not so secretly, apparently."

"I hoped maybe you felt the same way about me but didn't know how to deal with it. I was willing to wait however long it took."

"Excuse me while I go choke on the irony of it all." He rubbed his forehead with a sigh. "As you would say, we're a bunch of *feckin' eejits*, aren't we?"

"Looks that way. You've got my accent down, though. And it's kind of sexy and I don't know why."

Augie laughed. "As a connoisseur of Irish brogues, I try my best."

"A connoisseur?"

"With as many Irish people as I've been with, I've developed quite an ear for it."

His claim intrigued me. "Do tell."

"Fiona was from Belfast, but you have a Dundrum Dublin accent."

"How the hell do you know about Dundrum?" I

asked in shock. He knew I was from Dublin, but I had never mentioned a specific section of the city. It was pointless when no one in America was familiar enough with the area to know where the hell I was talking about.

He grinned at my reaction. "Sophomore year, I hooked up with an exchange student who sounded like you. She was a linguistics major, so when I commented on her Irish accent, she got very indignant and schooled me that there wasn't one monolithic Irish accent. When she realized I was genuinely interested in the subject, she explained the differences in regional dialects. She also pointed out there's not just one Dublin accent but a ton of them. After that, I started paying attention and learned to tell the difference."

Even with the explanation, it still baffled me. "Okay, but how could you pinpoint it being Dundrum when you've never been to Ireland?"

"I meant it when I said she sounded like you," he told me. "That was the reason I pursued her, plus she was cute as hell. She said Dundrum didn't sound the same as Finglas or Whitehall, but they were all grouped under the category of a Dublin accent. She told me hers was Dundrum specifically, so I assumed yours was, too."

"I'm impressed, not to mention a little turned on."

Augie's cheeks flushed an endearing shade of pink. "It makes sense when you think about it. People from Manhattan, the Bronx, and Brooklyn all sound different, even though it's all New York City. Same thing."

Unable to endure any longer, I stood and picked him up off the couch. He yelped in surprise and wrapped his arms around my neck as I carried him into my bedroom.

"You're so damn strong," he moaned, leaning into my hold. "We definitely need to have wall sex at some point."

I set him down next to my bed. "That's on my list, too."

Augie seemed intrigued. "You have a list?"

"A *very* long list." I peeled off my shirt before tossing it.

His eyes devoured me as he moved close enough to touch. He started at my chest, sliding his hands down in tandem over my sculpted body until he reached the button of my jeans. As he undid it and my zipper, he said, "We should compare them sometime." He then slid my pants and briefs off, which I kicked aside.

It was my turn to strip him. "Between the flight this morning and moving all your brother's stuff, I would suggest we start in the shower tonight."

"That sounds like an excellent idea." He followed me into my bathroom, where we got into the shower once the water was hot enough.

I pulled him closer for a kiss, loving our wet bodies

pressed together. My hands traced the path of the water down his back, then over the curve of his tight arse that I so adored. I would never take it for granted that he allowed me to be with him.

Augie moved away to pick up my shower puff, pouring some of my body wash onto it.

"Is that your subtle way of telling me I stink?"

"No, it's my very convenient excuse to touch you everywhere." He went from my shoulder down my left arm, leaving a trail of suds.

I enjoyed the experience of him washing me. He did my other arm before starting at my neck and over my chest, then down my torso. My prick was at full attention, but he skipped it in favor of doing each of my legs.

"Turn around."

I obeyed, but it took an effort not to pleasure myself as he worked up my legs, to my back, and finally my shoulders. Only then did he slide the puff back down to my arse. I spread my legs a little further apart when he teased me by rubbing against my perineum and bollocks. "You missed a spot."

"So impatient," he tutted. "Turn around."

I did so, my breath hitching at the sight of Augie on his knees in front of me. Memories of his mouth sucking my dick so expertly replayed in my mind, making me almost painfully hard.

He smirked like he knew where my thoughts had gone. Without a word, he washed my erection, taking care in pulling back my foreskin to clean me thoroughly. He then started jerking me off in the process of washing. I ached for something more substantial. When he stopped, I bit back a swear.

My complaints disappeared as he put on a show of bathing himself next. It was as if I was marking him with my scent, which my primal instincts loved. I behaved myself by not taking over like I wanted to, which became a significant challenge when he washed his intimate parts. "You know, I'd be happy to help with that, darlin'."

He smirked as he continued stroking himself. "Do you have some objection to watching?"

"Only that I'm dying to touch you."

"Fine, you can rinse me after you do yourself."

That would have to be enough. I pulled the showerhead from the holder and thoroughly rinsed off before doing him next. I made sure there was no trace of body wash suds remaining on him, before turning him around. When he exposed his back to me, I returned the wand to its holder. I embraced him from behind with both arms, then nuzzled against his neck, breathing in deep. "You smell good."

He chuckled. "I smell like you."

"I know, that's why." Powerless to resist temptation, I wrapped my hand around his hardness for a wank. "What I'd like right now is to ride you hard. How does that sound?"

"Like a great idea."

After I shut off the water, we toweled off before getting into bed. I lay down as Augie kissed me everywhere while preparing me. It was so good I almost expected to open my eyes and find out it was all a beautiful dream. Once I was ready, I rolled us over so I was on top. I stroked his prick to slick it with lube, causing him to make a confused noise.

"What about a condom?"

"None of my fantasies involved those," I replied with a laugh.

He wrinkled his brow. "But this is real life."

"Do I need one?"

"No, I'm good, but—"

I cut him off with an insistent kiss. "Augie, I won't be satisfied with anything less than all of you."

"Only if you're sure."

"I'm positively certain." I positioned myself over him and eased onto his lubed cock. It was a far better sensation than the unforgiving silicone dildo I had been using to practice. I loved how he gripped my splayed thighs, only loosening his hold when I was fully seated.

"Are you okay?"

I constricted my muscles around him, earning a delicious whimper from him. "I'm fucking fantastic."

With those words, I started moving in search of more pleasure. Whereas the dildo made you do all the work, Augie thrusted up with my every downward bounce and drove me wild. I tossed my head back with a moan as I worked up to a satisfying rhythm, loving how his hands caressed any part of me they could reach. As I grew more comfortable, I became more aggressive in my movements. I rode him with abandon as I lost myself in the sensations bombarding me.

When he jerked me off, the overload from the dual pleasure caused my pace to falter. He chuckled at that. "Not up to multitasking?"

I keened low in my throat as he kept working me, my pace becoming sporadic as I neared the apex of my limits.

"Fuck, you feel so good, Ambrose! I can't hold out much longer."

It sounded like he intended to pull out, which I wasn't interested in. "Good, because I want you come inside me."

"Oh, sweet merciful fuck!"

I leaned forward, gasping at what the change in angles did. It let him hit deeper, and I fucked him hard with a flurry of fractured swears.

He arched up as he came with a soft cry. His cum squirting inside me was like nothing else I had ever experienced. My whole body bowed as I orgasmed, marking his stomach with my seed. I braced myself on the bed, shaking from the intensity of my release, unable to move anymore. All I could do was whisper Augie's name in awe.

I lifted off his spent member, shivering when it

caused some of his cum to seep out of me. It made me feel like I was his. I couldn't believe he was finally mine and loved me as much as I loved him.

"Did I hurt you, or—"

"Everything was perfect," I reassured him. "I love you so much, Augie. So damn much."

"I love you, too, but you're *really* heavy."

With an apology kiss, I moved so he could curl up on me instead.

Satisfied with his position, he asked, "Was it everything you hoped it would be?"

"Actually, it proved I have an absolute shite imagination. That was a million times better than my fantasies." It astounded me that reality had exceeded my high expectations. When did that ever happen? "Thanks to you, poor Augusto is getting fired."

He snickered. "I can't believe you named your dildo *Augusto*. Like, did you moan 'Augusto' when you went to town on him?"

"Don't be daft." I ruffled his hair. "Your name is the only one I ever moaned. I think it gave Augusto a complex, but he doesn't talk, so it's fine."

"Out of curiosity, did you call me August or Augie?"

Busted, I fessed up. "I *may* have taken to calling you Augie in my fantasies. Sometimes I'd switch it up with a darlin' thrown in here and there. As a result, I've almost slipped up and called you by the wrong name a couple of times."

He laughed. "I should have guessed since you called me that around Sara and Fiona like you had done it a thousand times before."

"Oh, it's at least a million," I countered. "That's a rather conservative estimate, though."

"Wow, how much sex did you imagine us having?"

While it was embarrassing to say out loud, I owed him honesty. "It wasn't just sex. I would think about coming home after work and you'd kiss me hello. Or hugging you from behind while we made dinner, and you elbowing me to make me quit distracting you with kisses. When I would lick along the shell of your ear, you'd tell me if I didn't stop, zucchini wouldn't be the only thing you'd be cutting tonight."

He cracked up until tears came to his eyes. Once he reined in his reaction, he asked, "*That's* your fantasy? Me threatening you with bodily harm for being physically affectionate?"

"In your defense, the vegetables you were sautéing were in danger of being burned," I told him. "I'd hate for your effort to go to waste, so I'd back off for a bit."

"What would happen next?"

I brushed my thumb against his upper arm as I held him. "We would enjoy your delicious dinner while we talked about our day, what our brothers were up to, or made plans for the weekend. Then, I'd make love to you on the kitchen counter and you'd remind me this was my idea, so I'd be the one cleaning up afterward. I'd say it was a small price to pay to enjoy the pleasure of being with you. When we'd finish, you would supervise my cleanup and thank me with a kiss. After that, we'd cuddle on the couch with our cat before bed."

He repeated with surprise, "*Our* cat? You pictured us living together?"

"Like I'd let my husband live anywhere else," I scoffed, not realizing until too late what I had confessed.

He remained silent and unmoving, making me regret not keeping my damn gob shut. When he sat up, I had a momentary fear that he would leave in disgust. "Is that what you honestly want?"

I refused to run from my feelings for him anymore, so I owned up to the truth. "Someday, if I'm fortunate enough that that's what you want."

"You're serious?"

His disbelief was understandable given my history with never settling with anyone before. I reached up and stroked his cheek as I held his gaze. "With the utmost sincerity. I belong to you, Augie. I'm yours to do whatever you wish."

Tears welled up in his green eyes at my declaration. "How is that possible?"

"Because once I understood how much I loved you, I knew there would never be anyone else."

His voice wavered. "But what if I don't live up to the me inside your mind?"

"You're so much more than anything I've ever

imagined," I assured him. "Being with you for real is the true dream. Nothing will ever beat that."

"If this is a dream, I never want to wake up."

"You and me both, darlin'."

Augie bent down and kissed me sweetly as I cuddled him close, my heart full of more love and joy than I thought was possible.

Chapter Eleven

AUGIE

I HAD FANTASIZED about Ambrose fucking me against a wall for so many years that it hardly seemed real that it was happening. He positioned me with a practiced ease, holding me up like I weighed nothing. I wrapped my legs and arms around him as he supported me. After he entered me, he hefted me up a little higher to get a better angle.

"You good?" he asked.

"Absolutely amazing."

"Damn right you are."

With my ankles crossed under his ass, I didn't have many options for getting any kind of traction to move independently. My limited mobility meant I held on for the ride as Ambrose took full control and made me writhe on the wall in ecstasy. I laced my fingers through his hair, caressing him as he dominated my desires in an impressive show of strength. It was such a turn-on that he could effortlessly take me in such a way.

Primal lust overtook both of us as he ravaged me. I was practically purring with satisfaction with each fierce thrust. Surrendering to his control felt so good as he guided my hips to help maximize my enjoyment. I moaned and gasped his name, getting a thrill every time it inspired a primitive growl out of him. He worked me masterfully, driving me wild.

Confident I was safe in his grasp, I used my right hand to jerk off. It spiked my euphoria to a new level, causing me to arch off the wall with a soft keen.

Ambrose compensated for my repositioning, never breaking his rhythm as he kept pounding into me. His voice was a dark rumble as he ordered, "Put on a show for me, darlin'."

Happy to do as he commanded, I grew increasingly vocal while I masturbated, calling out to him as I overwhelmed myself from the intensity of the experience. "Ambro—*oh, fuck!*"

"That's it, let me hear you."

More than willing to oblige, I was grateful he had a house and not an apartment. Otherwise, his neighbor would have been banging against the other side of the wall and yelling at us to keep it down.

My toes curled as I got closer, my grip in his hair tightening as I raced toward my finish. I was almost there when his phone rang.

He didn't stop for it, but when they called back

again, he growled in irritation. The third try made him angrily swear up a storm. After the fourth time, I suggested, "Maybe you should answer. It's obviously important."

When his ringtone sounded a fifth time, it caused him to pull out with a flurry of very creative Irish curses. He lowered me to stand and went over to answer it with a snarl. "You've got my bloody attention! What the fuck do you want?"

All traces of rage disappeared in an instant as Ambrose asked, "Cally?" He pulled the phone from his ear to check the number. "Where are you calling me from?" He listened to the reply, his eyebrows furrowing in confusion. "What? Why? Is everything okay?"

Whatever Ambrose's younger brother Callum said caused him to grow even more concerned. After a pause, he gave his address. "I can come—are you sure? I'd feel better if—all right. I'll see you soon." He hung up with a frown.

"Callum's here?" Given how close the brothers were, it seemed unusual that Ambrose didn't know about his arrival.

"Yeah, but he won't tell me why." He had gone soft from worrying. "He sounded really upset, though. None of this makes sense. Cally's never been a spur-of-the-moment kind of kid. He hates surprises."

"There has to be a reason."

"Not a single good one I can think of," he said.

"Showing up at the airport without any warning or even my address is so out of character for him. I don't like this."

I hugged him to offer what comfort I could. "I'm confident he'll tell you everything when he gets here."

He relaxed into my embrace as he held me. "Sorry it wrecked the moment."

I kissed the underside of Ambrose's chin. "Making sure he's okay is much more important. If anyone understands that, it's me. As many times as you've put up with canceling our plans last minute because something happened with Felix, I'm not in any position to get upset about it."

Ambrose held me tighter. "I promise I'll make it up to you later."

"I know you will." Even though I hated doing it, I pulled away to get ready to leave to give the brothers their privacy for their reunion.

He watched me getting dressed and sighed heavily. "You have no idea how much it's breaking my heart that you have to go."

"We'll have plenty of chances to finish this later. You should be there for your brother."

Ambrose began putting his clothes back on with a discontented grumble. "It doesn't mean I have to be happy about it."

When he finished, I kissed him goodbye. "I'm not, either, but he gets a pass this time."

He walked me to the foyer. "Thanks for understanding, Augie."

"You would do the same for me if it was Felix," I reminded him. "That's what being an overprotective big brother means."

Ambrose pinned me against the door as he plundered my mouth in a passionate goodbye. It reignited the embers of my earlier arousal, so I gently pushed him back. We didn't have time for that. "Please stop making it harder to leave."

"Sorry."

I gave him a chaste kiss. "Let me know how everything goes later."

"Will do."

He stole one more lingering kiss before I left.

Chapter Twelve

AMBROSE

CALLUM'S sudden appearance didn't sit well with me. It was so unlike him to show up without warning. We had talked about him coming out to Sunnyside to visit me at some point, but that was always with a sense of excitement. He had sounded so small and sad on the phone that I couldn't stop worrying about what happened.

When I opened the door, my gut twisted at the sight of my beautiful baby brother staring downcast with a black eye and a single duffle bag. Instead of wearing his normal dressy clothes and bow tie, he had on jeans and one of my old hoodies that dwarfed him. "C'mere, Cally," I encouraged him, holding my arms out to him.

He hesitated before he entered my house and hugged me with a sob. I held him tighter as he wept, baffled and concerned by his reaction. He sounded like he was in so much pain that it tore at my heart. I soothed him as best as I could, letting him take as much time as he needed. Whenever he tried to apologize, I shushed him. "Let it all out. You're safe here."

It took a while for his cries to subside into sniffles, but I refused to release him until he pulled away. He stepped back to wipe his tears, looking like he could cry sixteen thousand more. I was ready to kill whoever had hurt him so badly. "I'm sorry, Brody." Only my family used that nickname for me. It always made me feel a little nostalgic for home.

"You're fine." Leaving his stuff in the hall, I guided him to my living room and told him to make himself comfortable on the couch. I grabbed him some water from the kitchen, handing it to him before sitting next to him.

His hands trembled as he opened the bottle and took a small sip. He set it aside, unable to meet my gaze.

I reached out to touch his face, marred by the ugly bruise. He jerked away from me, almost as if he feared I would strike him. Not taking it personally, I kept my voice gentle. "Who did this to you?"

He was silent for so long that I almost thought he wouldn't answer me. "Gregory."

Things made even less sense now. The two of them were inseparable childhood best friends. Gregory had spent so much time at our house growing up that he felt like another younger brother to me. I couldn't imagine gentle Gregory raising his hand to Callum, let alone leaving him with such a nasty black eye. "What happened?"

Tears sprung to Callum's eyes again, but they didn't fall. "If I tell you, I'll have nowhere else to go."

"There's nothing you could ever say or do that would make me turn you away," I insisted. "Absolutely nothing, you hear me?"

"I wish I could believe that."

The lack of faith in me was hurtful, but I understood it stemmed from whatever had happened to him and wasn't personal. "Cally, I mean it. Nothing'll ever change that."

"This will," he said with quiet conviction. "You'll hate me, too."

"Listen to me and listen good. I promise I'll always love you, no matter what."

The despair in his eyes was gut-wrenching as he whispered, "Even if I'm gay?"

Everything came into sharp focus. I felt sick to my stomach realizing that if he was here, our dad had disowned and banished him. It confirmed all my fears about not having a home if I came out to my parents as bisexual. Pushing aside my reaction, I focused on making sure he knew he was safe and loved. "*Especially* then."

"It doesn't disgust you?"

He was too fragile for me to tell him that not only

did it not disgust me, but I was bollocks-deep in my boyfriend when he called. "Not in the least."

"Really?"

I couldn't blame him for his disbelief. We were raised in the same house with the same religion, so as far as he was aware, I shared our parents' views. "Really. If you have a boyfriend, he's welcome here. You never need to hide who you love from me. Not now, not ever."

Callum hid his face in his hands with a relieved sob. "I was so scared you would shun me, too."

It stirred up my guilt that my previous behavior had hurt my brother, whom I adored, but it wasn't the time to dwell on that. I reached and rubbed his back in comfort. "I'm sorry, I never meant to harm you that way."

He looked up with a sniffle. "It's not your fault. I just thought because of Da and church—"

"I've learned a lot since I left Ireland, including how wrong and hateful they were. I renounced their bigoted views a long time ago. You have nothing to fear from me. Gay, bi, straight, asexual, whatever— none of that would ever make me love you any less. I love you as you are, Cally. You never have to question that. You always have a home with me."

Callum threw himself on me in another hug, shaking from the force of his emotions. "Thank you, Brody."

I tried to lighten his mood a little by teasing him.

"Don't be daft. You shouldn't thank me for loving you when it's the easiest thing in the world for me to do."

It drew a soft chuckle out of him, as I hoped it would, but he quickly grew somber as he sat back. "It didn't matter to Da. He said he refused to live with a sodomite sinner under his roof and threw me out. He told me not to return until I was willing to love a woman as the Lord intended."

"Oh, Cally. I'm so sorry." It devastated me that our dad banished sweet, beautiful Callum for being gay. It made me want to get on the next flight to Dublin and have words with him, none of which would be nice.

He took a sip of water before he added, "Ma tried to stop him."

That came as a genuine surprise. "She did?"

"It shocked me, too." His wry smile slid into sadness. "She told him if God didn't want me to be gay, he wouldn't have made me that way. You can well imagine what he said to that. She insisted disowning me was an un-Christianly thing to do, but he wouldn't listen. He stormed out of the house and warned I better not be there when he got back from the pub or else. I wasn't sure what else to do, so I started packing."

"I can't believe she stood up to him." Ma rarely defied our father, preferring not to fight over the nasty yelling.

"While I packed, Ma applied online for that

waiver thing you need to come to America for ninety days on my behalf, which was approved immediately. After that, she booked me a ticket here on the next plane and gave me her credit card. She apologized for not being able to do more than that, but she feared Da would hurt me if I stayed. Ma knew I would be safe with you."

That was so much more than I ever would have expected our pacifist mother to do under those circumstances. I patted Callum on the back. "You did the right thing coming here."

"I can really stay here?"

"Absolutely," I promised. "You're mad if you think I'm sending you back to Da after that."

"I don't know what I'll do after the ninety days are up, but—"

My brain was already working on plans on how to keep my brother here long-term. "My friend Rhys owns his own company. When he returns from his honeymoon, I'll talk to him and see if maybe he can hire you and secure a work visa. It's probably the fastest way to make that happen."

"Do you think he'd be willing to help?"

"I know he will. He's a great guy and would treat you well if you worked for him."

"So, I wouldn't have to go back to Ireland?" He sounded hopeful for the first time since his arrival.

As much as I wanted to say yes, it wasn't as simple as that. "You may need to return temporarily for a new visa, but you won't be going alone. I'll stay with you over there as long as it takes until you can come back here. While we're there, I'll also pick up anything you couldn't bring with you. You don't have to deal with Da ever again."

He sagged against the couch with a sigh, finally relaxing. "That's such a relief."

"Once you get a little more settled, we can turn the guest room into your room," I told him. "Whatever you want, you can do. This is your home now."

"No, I don't deserve that."

"You're right—you deserve more. But we'll start there and figure things out, okay?"

"Okay."

I got off the couch and gestured for him to follow me. "Come on, let's get you upstairs for a shower and some rest. It's been a long day for you."

"Thank you for this, for everything."

"There's nothing I wouldn't do for you. I love you, Cally."

When he smiled, he looked more like the Callum I knew. It gave me hope that things would work out for him.

Chapter Thirteen

AUGIE

IT HAD BEEN three days since Callum's arrival. As much as I wished to give the brothers their time together, I couldn't help but feel a little neglected. Ambrose hadn't given me a single update about what happened, which was unusual. Not wanting to be obtrusive, I settled for texting a casual "How's it going?"

When he finally called me, I tried not to sound too eager when I answered the phone. "Hey."

"Mm, it's good to hear your voice again, darlin'."

While the petty part of me wanted to point out he was the reason it had been so long since we had talked, I kept things light. "I literally said one word."

"Yeah, but I missed you."

His genuine longing disarmed my previous irritation over the lack of communication between us the past few days. It made it easier to admit the truth. "I missed you, too. I've been worried."

He sighed heavily, and I could picture him running his fingers through his beautiful auburn hair. "I'm sorry, Augie. I've been so busy dealing with Cally that time got away from me."

"Is there anything I can do?"

"Forgive me for letting everything get all arse-ways?" he asked.

"As long as you don't make it a habit. Are you at least having fun with your brother?"

"Yeah, it's been great catching up with him," he said. "We've had some great talks that have been a long time coming."

"Did you tell him about us?"

Ambrose hesitated. "Not yet."

That wasn't the answer I expected three days into Callum's visit. "Oh."

He hurried to explain himself. "There were other things we needed to deal with first. It just isn't the right time yet."

It sounded like an excuse to me. "Okay."

"I will when the moment is right, though," he promised.

Something told me I'd be waiting a long, long time for that to happen. Despite all of Ambrose's big talk, faced with the reality of telling his brother about our relationship, it turned out he was too much of a coward to tell the truth. It was hard not to choke on my bitter disappointment. "Sounds good. I'll let you get back to him."

"Augie—"

I didn't allow him to finish his sentence. "Talk to you later."

Before he could say anything else, I ended the call and tossed my phone onto the coffee table with a frustrated growl. The shame Ambrose felt over being with me cut me deep. I didn't want to be his dirty little secret that he hid from his family, but it looked like that was all I'd ever be. Foolishly, I had bought into his declarations of love and believed him when he said he wanted to be with me openly. I should have known better. Things never worked out so perfectly for me.

Curling up on my couch with a miserable sigh, I was officially the world's biggest idiot.

"AUGIE."

I opened my eyes, squinting at the sudden brightness. Momentarily disoriented from my unintentional afternoon nap, I blinked in confusion at the sight of Ambrose sitting on my coffee table. He had a key to my apartment, but it wasn't like him to come in unannounced. "Mm?"

He looked down at me with concern. "We need to talk." The words made my heart sink because a breakup always followed them. My fear must have shown on my face. He hurried to clarify, "Not that kind of talk. Please hear me out."

With a sigh, I struggled to sit upright and was touched to discover he had covered me up with a blanket. I pulled it tighter around me as I sighed. "Fine."

"Cally's not here on vacation. He's moving in with me."

"Really?"

"Da threw him out of the house permanently," Ambrose explained. "Cally had nowhere else to go."

I knew Callum was a good kid, so I couldn't imagine what he could have done to cause his father to banish him. "What happened?"

"Cally's best friend found out he was gay and gave him a black eye over it."

The information about the assault horrified me. "What the fuck kind of friend does that?"

"One raised in a strict Irish Catholic family," Ambrose said with a frown. "When Cally went home, our parents interrogated him about the bruise. He told them the truth, and Da immediately disowned him, telling him to never come back."

My heart twisted at hearing the cruel reaction. It made Ambrose's fear about not having a family if he came out as bisexual even more real. "Shit, I'm so sorry. There aren't enough words for how awful that is."

"He didn't know what else to do, so he packed his

stuff and came here." Ambrose dropped his gaze as he wrung his hands. "He was so scared to tell me what happened, because he thought I'd hate and shun him, too."

I did my best to reassure him. "After your dad's reaction, it's completely understandable. You can't blame yourself for that. It sounds like he's been through hell and back."

Ambrose's guilt was all over his handsome face. "I should have done a better job of letting him know that he could come to me about anything. It's my fault for not making sure he understood he never had to hide that part of himself from me. It kills me I hurt him with all the cruel things I used to say out of ignorance."

I reached out and took his hands in mine to force him to look at me. "The important thing is that he knows now that he has a safe place with you to be himself, always."

His remorse tugged at my heartstrings. "That's why I couldn't say anything to him yet. He was still processing his trauma over losing his best friend and Da over being gay. He needed to be in a better head-space before I drop my bombshell that I'm bi with a sexy boyfriend. That's what I meant by it wasn't the right time. It's not because I'm ashamed of being with you, Augie. I just wanted to give him a little longer to gather his bearings, you know?"

"I'm sorry I overreacted," I apologized. "I

shouldn't have assumed you didn't want to tell Callum because you're embarrassed of me."

Ambrose moved to sit next to me on the couch. "I'm nothing but proud of you, Augie. I love you so much, and I want him to know that. And when I return to Ireland with him in a few months for his visa, I'll tell my parents, too. I'm done hiding who I am."

His words moved me, but I still worried. "You'll lose your family, though."

"I wrote Da out of my life the minute he tossed Cally on the streets," he said. "What use is his approval when he'll do that to my sweet baby brother? Fuck him."

"But what about your mom?"

"She tried to stand up for Cally, which I never expected. Not only that, but she bought him his plane ticket here and gave him her credit card. She's checked in with me a few times to see if he's okay."

The news was heartening. "I'm glad she didn't write him off, too."

"It at least made me feel better knowing that Ma trusted I wouldn't turn him away because he's gay." He looked up at me with a beseeching plea in his beautiful blue eyes. "Would you come home with me so we can tell Cally about us?"

"Are you sure you want me there for that conversation? Maybe that's something for the two of you to do in private before he meets me."

Ambrose said, "He knows who you are. I've told him a million stories about you over the years."

"Yes, but there's an enormous difference between knowing me as your best friend August versus your boyfriend Augie."

"I really want you there with me when I tell him, so please," he requested.

"Only if you're sure."

"I'm definitely sure." He leaned in and claimed my lips in a kiss that left no doubt in my mind about how serious he was. "I'm also sure I'd like to finish what we started the other day before he interrupted us."

My dick perked up at the invitation. "Oh?"

"Interested?"

I pretended to think about it long enough to make him nervous, before answering with a grin. "Always."

"Good." Without wasting another second, he swept me off the couch into his arms to carry me back to my bedroom.

I laughed as I held on, looking forward to him asserting his love for me again.

Chapter Fourteen

AMBROSE

AS MUCH AS I enjoyed finishing our fuck against the wall without interruption, snuggling in bed afterward was my favorite part of the afternoon. I loved being able to cuddle with Augie afterward, holding him in my arms as we talked about everything and nothing.

After more sexy times in the shower to make up for lost time, we arrived back at my house. I hoped Callum wouldn't get upset about how long I'd hidden my sexuality from him. It was yet another thing to curse our father over. I focused on being grateful we could finally move beyond the damage he had inflicted on us since childhood.

When we entered, I called out to Callum, "I'm back, and I brought someone."

He sat in the living room chair, where he had been reading a book to pass the time while I was at Augie's apartment. In high spirits, he wore black slacks and a blue shirt with one of his favorite bow ties instead of a hoodie and sweats. "Welcome home!" His smile brightened when he saw Augie. "You must be August."

"That would be me." He reached out to shake my brother's hand. "It's nice to meet you in person."

"I've heard so many stories about you I almost feel like we're already friends," Callum told him as we sat down on my dark green sofa.

"Oh, good, so it's not just me."

Not wanting to put it off any longer, it was best to jump straight into the conversation we needed to have. "There's something important I've been wanting to talk to you about for a while now."

He set his book aside to give me his full attention.

"I intended to tell you during my next visit back home, but…" With a deep breath, I confessed. "August—Augie—isn't just my best friend. He's also my boyfriend."

Callum's gaze darted back and forth between us. "Your *boyfriend*? Like, your *boyfriend*-boyfriend? You mean just a friend who's a boy, right?"

I took Augie's hand in mine and interlaced our fingers to bring it up to place a kiss on the back of it. "No, I mean Augie's my dating-the-greatest-love-of-my-life boyfriend."

There were several fractured syllables as Callum tried to form words in response. "B-but you're straight! How can *you* of all men be gay?"

"Actually, I'm bisexual."

Callum looked shell-shocked by the revelation. "*You're* bi? *You*? Seriously, Brody? How?" He continued spluttering. "I mean, you're *you*. With all those women, I…"

"Over the years, I realized I wanted more than that. Now that I'm with Augie, I've never been happier," I told him. "My biggest regret is that I wasted so many years ignoring how I felt about him, hoping it would go away. I spent too much time being ashamed of something that wasn't wrong."

My brother smiled sadly. "That I understand all too well. It's exhausting."

"I'm sorry I didn't tell you sooner. If I had, you would have known you could come to me earlier without fear."

He brushed his fingers over the bruise by his eye. "I never imagined you of all people would have a boyfriend." The corner of Callum's mouth turned upward in a grin. "Well, I guess your comment about me being welcome to bring a guy over here wasn't just empty words."

"I sincerely meant it," I promised. "I'm done hiding who I am anymore, and you shouldn't, either. You should be you."

"Thank you, Brody."

It didn't surprise me when Augie offered, "Once you're more settled, I can introduce you to my younger brother, Felix. He goes to college near here and has a wonderful group of friends around your age."

"That's very kind, but I wouldn't have much in common with them. I'm not much for parties."

"They're all out and proud, whose idea of a good night is chatting in PJs over ice cream while watching a movie." Augie chuckled at my brother's surprised expression. "They aren't the 'hit the clubs and get wasted' type if that's what you're worried about."

I reminded him, "You've heard me talk about Felix before. He'd be a great friend to you."

"Once my shiner goes away, I think I'd enjoy that. It'd be nice to have friends again."

"Agreed," I added. "Is anyone else ready for dinner?"

My brother questioned, "Would you get annoyed if we ordered Mexican again? I'm obsessed with that cinnamon and vanilla rice milk drink. What was it called again?"

"Horchata. You can thank Augie for introducing me to it."

His boyish enthusiasm was precious. "Oh, it's the best thing ever!"

"You know what's better than horchata?" Augie asked.

"Nothing?" he guessed with a laugh.

"A horchata milkshake."

Callum lit up with delight. "I never even thought

of that! Oh, I bet that would be *amazing*. Please, Brody? Can we?"

I pulled out my phone to place an order online. "It's fine with me. What do you want this time?"

He cheered before telling me what he wanted for dinner. My spirits soared at seeing him so happy again.

CALLUM HAD COME out of his shell talking with Augie during dinner. It was beautiful seeing the two of them bonding and having such a good time together. After dinner, we watched a movie together while enjoying our horchata milkshakes, which were indeed delicious. It was truly a perfect evening. I couldn't wait for more nights like that together.

When my brother crashed from his still-lingering jet lag, I drove Augie back home. Once inside his apartment, I hugged him tightly. "Thanks for tonight."

"Movie night was a lot of fun." He snuggled closer into my hold. "By the way, it's super cute he calls you Brody."

"It's a family nickname."

"I like it. Also, I see why he reminds you of Felix. In five minutes, they'll be best friends forever."

"Nothing would make me happier."

He looked up at me with an impish grin. "Oh, I

could think of one or two things that might make you happier than that." He guided me down for a heated kiss, opening for me to indulge in the sweet taste of his mouth. "It looks like you've got the right idea."

"I love how you think." We stripped out of our clothes as we walked to his room, completely bare by the time we fell into bed together. I won the battle for top, pinning him under me. When he ran his fingers through my hair in a gentle caress as he held on to me, I melted under his touch. "Do you have any idea how much I want you?"

"You have me, so take me."

Not needing to be told twice, I showered him in kisses while stretching him open with a patience I didn't have. It was worth it to be buried to the hilt in him, loving how his body welcomed me. There was no better feeling than sliding in his slicked, tight channel in the most intimate of embraces. I lost myself in the ecstasy of moving together. Having him hold on to me with soft whimpers and moans of plea-sure was one of life's greatest pleasures. I loved making him cry out my name as he arched from the overwhelming sensations. Truly, I was the luckiest man alive.

It only took a few touches to make him come with a loud keen. I pushed deep into him as I followed suit, deriving great satisfaction from marking him as mine that way. He pulled me closer for a hungry kiss, and I gladly surrendered myself to him forever.

WHEN I RETURNED AFTER MIDNIGHT, it surprised me to see Callum curled up on the couch in his green flannel pajamas under a blanket. Before I left, he had been getting ready for bed.

He glanced up from his book when I drew closer and greeted me. "Welcome home!"

I sat down next to him. "Thanks. Is everything okay?"

"Yeah. I was exhausted, but I couldn't fall asleep. Instead of tossing and turning, I came back down to read."

"Do you want to talk about what's keeping you up, or would you prefer I left you alone?"

Callum didn't answer right away. He used his thumb to fan the pages of the book a couple of times, before he set it aside on the coffee table. It took him some time before he asked me, "When did you know?"

"That I liked Augie?"

"Guys in general."

I ruffled my hair with a sigh. "If I'm being honest with myself, it goes back to when I was a teenager. I'd pretend not to notice that my gaze lingered on men a little longer than it should have. When I got aroused from skinny-dipping with Donnelly, I knew damn well it was because he was fucking gorgeous, wet, and naked. However, I desperately lied to myself that it was only from the thrill of potentially getting caught."

Callum's cheeks flushed. "I had such a big crush on him when I was younger."

"Everyone did, including me." My childhood best friend had become a famous model, surprising no one given how handsome he was. "Sometimes I would have thoughts about him or men working out at the gym that very much went against the Church's teaching. I'd burn with shame and pretend it never happened. After a while, I became very good at ignoring my urges by living in deep denial."

"How did you come to terms with it?"

I grinned. "Augie didn't give me a choice. He worked his way into my heart without even trying. There was a lot of self-loathing and anger at first, but I couldn't run away from how much I desired him. Eventually, it became normal to want him. It was when I realized I wanted more than just sex that I understood how real my feelings for him were. I stopped hating myself and took a chance on happiness with him instead. I haven't looked back since."

Callum straightened the blanket over his knees. "You really love him, don't you?"

"More than I ever realized was possible," I answered without a second of hesitation. "I regret all the years I wasted running away from something this wonderful."

He glanced at me with curiosity. "But don't you miss girls?"

"They're fun, but the physical gratification I get with them is nothing compared to the connection I have with him. I don't need anyone else when I have him to love."

"Wow." Callum looked amazed by my declaration, which was understandable given my history. "Who would have thought my womanizer playboy brother would end up with a boyfriend? Da will lose his mind when he finds out."

"Let him. I've already wasted too much of my life hating who I am because of him. He can rot as far as I care."

Callum was quiet for a long moment as he gathered the courage to speak. "It bothers me he probably thinks I've sucked every dick in Dublin and fucked any man who's looked at me. All I've ever done is go to a gay bar last week. I haven't even had a boyfriend or my first kiss yet."

I arched my eyebrows at the information. "You actually went to one? But you hate pubs."

"I can handle a pub, just not a club." His words gave me a flashback to dancing with Augie in the Las Vegas club, but I pushed it aside. "It was the only place I felt safe enough to explore."

The thought of sweet, naïve Callum going to a pub in search of meaningless affection pained me, but I didn't comment on it. "What happened?"

His cheeks burned almost as red as his hair. "A guy gave me his number, but I was too scared to call him. I didn't want my first time to be like that."

"There's nothing wrong with that. It's so much better with someone who cares about you."

Callum nudged some wrinkles out of the blanket, unable to look at me. "Not all of us are lucky enough to have our best friend love us back."

My heart broke for my brother. "I'm so sorry."

He touched the edge of his bruise. "I was an idiot for thinking Gregory could ever feel that way about me."

"No, that's not—"

"It is true!"

There was more I could say, but he wasn't ready to listen. "That didn't give him any right to hit you. I could kill him for that."

"It's my fault for telling him I had a crush on him."

I refused to let my brother blame himself. "Don't you dare make excuses for him hurting you. What he did was wrong and unforgivable. None of this was your fault, Cally."

"When he brought up that Craig saw me at the gay bar, I really thought he was going to tell me he was gay, too." Callum sighed as he ran his hand through his hair. "There's no point dwelling on it now, though. What's done is done. I need to move on."

"Felix and his friends will help," I promised. "They're good lads."

His smile was self-deprecating as he joked, "I'll try not to fall in love with any of them."

"You'll love who you're meant to be with." I ruffled his hair. "Come on, it's late. You should get some sleep."

"Yeah, you're right." Callum stood up and folded the blanket neatly to set back on the couch. He had always been fastidious. "Thank you for introducing me to August. I enjoyed getting to know him tonight."

It was a relief that he liked Augie, although I never doubted it. "I'm glad. I didn't want there to be any more secrets between us."

"Oh, there's no secret about how you feel for him. It's obvious how much you love him."

"With all of my heart."

Callum hugged me good night. "Thanks for talking to me about everything, Brody."

"I'm sorry it took me so long to be honest with you. I shouldn't have let my fear of Da stop me from telling you the truth."

He tilted his head as he studied me. "Does Ma know?"

"If she does, she has the world's best poker face." I laughed at the notion. "Why?"

"I wondered if maybe that was why she sent me here to be with you."

His leap in logic made sense, although it wasn't

true. "No, I've never talked to her about it. But she understands that I would move heaven and earth to keep you safe. She's texted me every day asking for updates on how you're doing and if I'm feeding you enough. Ma would kill me if she knew I was letting you live on takeout. I can cook, you know."

"But takeout is such a rare treat!" He chuckled before growing somber again. "What was weird is she wasn't surprised at all when I came out. She was with us every Sunday at church and made sure we said our prayers, but she didn't seem disgusted or horrified at all. I don't get it."

It surprised me she had reacted in such a way. Then again, she was our kinder and more reasonable parent. "You've always been her special baby boy. She loves you with all of her heart. I'm glad that's still true. It gives me hope."

"I feel like a terrible son for assuming she'd reject me the way Da did. She really fought to protect me, but he wasn't having any of it." Tears gathered in his eyes. "I was so scared he would hurt her when he came home drunk from the pub. It would be my fault if he—"

"Hey," I gently interrupted him, squeezing his shoulder in silent support. "Stop blaming yourself. She's okay. I can show you her texts."

"But she's stuck there alone with him. You know how he gets when he drinks. And now…"

I couldn't blame him for getting upset. The

thought also turned my stomach, but I put on a brave face for his sake. "Ma doesn't take shite from anyone, least of all him. She hates fighting, but we've both seen her hand him his bollocks more than once. If you're worried, you can talk to her yourself. She sent you here because she wanted you to be safe, not because she never wanted to see you again."

"I wanted to text her, but I feared Da would punish her for being in contact with me."

"Forget about him. Send her a message in the morning. It'll make her day, trust me."

He squared his shoulders with new resolve. "I'll do that."

I guided him toward the stairs. "You should sleep, though. It's late."

After another hug, we headed upstairs to prepare for bed.

Chapter Fifteen

AUGIE

FEW THINGS WERE BETTER than following up a sexy Saturday morning with a lazy afternoon relaxing in bed. Curled up with Ambrose in a postcoital haze, life was perfect. I wasn't sure how I had gotten so lucky, but I was grateful to be living out my best fantasies with him.

His voice drew me from my distraction. "You know what we should do?"

"Stay right here and not move until we absolutely have to?"

He caressed my shoulder, raising chills on my skin. How was it even the tiniest touch from him made me want him more? It was extra impressive given how thoroughly he had pleasured me earlier in the morning.

"We should play strip poker."

Out of all the ideas he could have proposed, that

hadn't been an option I expected. I snickered at the absurdity of it. "There's a slight flaw in your plan: I'm already naked."

His hand moved from my shoulder down my back to allow him to squeeze my ass. The rumble of his voice sent shivers racing through me as he said, "Oh, I'm well aware of that fact. I meant later, though."

"You realize you don't need to play a game to get me naked, right? With your sexy accent, I'm pretty sure if you recited the alphabet, I'd be completely naked by the letter *F*—for fuck, naturally."

He laughed heartily at my comment. "You'd really be able to hold out to *F*?"

"Hey, I said I'd be *completely* naked by *F*," I defended myself. "I'd be immediately horny by *A* for Ambrose. I'd take my jacket off for *B*, thinking of you saying bollocks. Hearing *C* for cock would make my shirt disappear. My pants would definitely come off at *D* for dick. The socks would have to go with *E* for erotic. Obviously, the underwear would get stripped off with *F* for fuck, leaving me *fully* naked."

"So, *G* would be for get in bed?"

"Oh, absolutely," I agreed. "How about *H* for hold me down? Hard-on would work, too."

Between his answering rumble of approval and the topic, I grew erect again. His hand strayed downwards once again, his fingers running along the crack of my ass to tease my entrance. "*I* for insert fingers, perhaps?"

It was zero percent surprising to discover that Ambrose was already hard. I capitalized on the advantage it gave me by demonstrating my next suggestion. "*J* for jacking off."

"*K* for…"

I kept stroking his dick, enjoying making this more difficult for him. "Come on, that's an easy one."

"Not when you're doing that," he growled, but it didn't stop me from continuing.

I readjusted my position so I could lean closer to him. "*K* for kiss," I answered for him, then captured his lips in a passionate one. When we parted, I smirked. "*K* could also be for kink."

Ambrose rolled us over so he was now pinning me down to the bed. He ran his tongue along the curve of my neck. "*L* for lick."

I took myself in hand to give myself some relief while also providing another example. "*M* for masturbate."

"Hey, that's cheating! You already did jack off."

"On *you*." I put on a show of touching myself. "*This* is *me* masturbating."

He huffed in annoyance. "It's a cheap win."

"It's a win all the same," I countered. "I guess I could always go with manhood if you find it that objectionable. However, it sounds to me like you can't think of a word for *N*, and you're stalling for time."

"I'm not!"

To push his buttons, I scoffed. "Uh-huh, whatever you say."

"*N* is..." he tried to say, only to trail off again as he watched me pleasuring myself. "Damn it!"

I was having entirely too much fun with the game. "I'm sorry, am I distracting you?" I ran my thumb over the head of my cock, spreading the bead of precum. For good measure, I arched my back with a breathy moan. "Is *this* making it too hard to think?"

"Yes! Fuck it, pass."

"*N* for naked and naughty." I impishly added, "Or nasty, depending how you like to do it. Can you manage *O*, or do I need to do that one, too?"

"*O*—" he said, before cutting himself off. He reached down and moved my hand away to make me stop touching myself. "Fuck, I can't concentrate with you doing that!"

I preened in victory. "Too much to handle?"

He toyed with my arousal, telling me, "Oh, I can *more* than handle you."

"You're welcome to as soon as you tell me what *O* stands for."

"*O* is for oh, dear god, I fucking want you so much," he replied, then kissed me hard. "And orgasm. Can't forget that one."

I laughed at the response, but he resorted to an underhanded play by stroking both of our cocks together in his large hand. It felt divine, but I still had the wherewithal to answer, "*P* for pricks, penis, prostate, take your pick."

"*Q*—oh, come on! Why do I keep getting all the fucking hard ones?"

"Because you keep skipping." I laughed at his annoyed huffed. "I can't wait to see you figure out this one."

"There are no *Q*s in sex," he complained.

"You're just mad because I'm kicking your ass at this game."

Ambrose slid slicked fingers inside of me, simultaneously prepping me and attempting to distract me from winning. Too bad it wouldn't work. "Damn it, I could have said lube for *L*!"

"Too late now."

He remained defiant. "I bet you don't know a *Q*-related sex word, either."

"Sure I do," I told him. "You're going to feel like an idiot for not thinking of it first."

"You're lying!"

"No, you'll definitely kick yourself for missing something this obvious."

He accused me, "You're bluffing."

With great joy, I answered, "*Q* for quickie."

"Fuck!"

Grinning, I said, "I told you you'd feel stupid."

"Fuck quickies. You may as well not even have sex at that point! It barely counts!"

"I'll remind you of that the next time you try to

squeeze one in." Getting him riled up was too easy. "Anyway, where were we? So, *R*. Racy, raunchy, ravish, romantic, rough—should I go on, or are you ready to admit defeat yet?"

"No!" Bless his competitive nature. He withdrew his fingers from inside me, then stroked his impressive member with lube. He pushed into me, waiting until he was buried to the hilt to say triumphantly, "*S* for sex!"

"And he's back in the game, folks!"

He arrogantly said, "Don't count me out yet! I can still win this."

"How? You're down by three. We're running out of alphabet."

"I'll win by any means necessary." To prove his point, he moved in earnest.

Unfortunately for him, that just gave me ideas for a longer list of sex words starting with the letter *T*. "Ha, fat chance. Let's see, for *T* that could be take me hard, tease me, tent in your pants, testicles if you get to be technical about it, titillating, tumescent, turgid—"

He interrupted me with a hard thrust that caused me to cry out with lust. "What do those last two have to do with sex?"

"They're both gross adjectives for erections," I replied. "I'll wait if you want to look it up in the dictionary and prove I'm right. Now, can you come up with anything for *U*?"

To make it harder for him, I started stroking my hardness while using my other hand to toy with one of my nipples. There was a blazing need in his blue eyes as they drank me in, which made me hot all over. I whimpered Ambrose's name, pleading for more. Sure, it was manipulative, but it was also fun. When he only growled in response, I prompted him, "*U*?"

He was silent for several more thrusts before he admitted defeat. "Fuck it. '*U*' win. Satisfied?"

"Yes!" I moaned, the victory making the sex even better. But it wouldn't be a total win until I finished the game. "*U* for urges, up your ass—"

He barked a laugh. "*Really?*"

"Why not?" I shrugged. "*V* for vibrator or vigorous."

Ambrose obliged me with a demonstration of the latter with a thrust that curled my toes as I cried out. My mind awash with pleasure, it took a moment to compose myself enough to continue. "*W* would be wank, whack off, wanting, wang, wood—"

"Fine, fine, I've got the picture," Ambrose told me.

I drew a blank for *X* until I came up with "X-rated."

"That doesn't count!"

Not willing to concede my point, I challenged, "And what would you call this? PG-13? Please. X-rated totally works for *X*."

"Okay, then what about *Y*?"

"That's another easy one."

He scowled at that. "It's really not. There's not a single Y-word that's appropriate for this bizarre sex alphabet of yours."

"You," I answered. "Because I'm sure as hell not fucking anyone else."

"Damn right you're not." He kissed me until I was breathless.

I took advantage of the slowdown to reverse our positions once more to be on top of him. It allowed me to bounce down harder in search of pleasure, my back bowing from the intense sensations flooding through me.

"Is Z for zero, because that's how many sex words start with that letter?" Ambrose asked.

After making it that far, I refused to be defeated on the last letter of the damn alphabet. But when he started working my cock, I got lost in the pleasure. Overloaded on sexual ecstasy, coherent thinking became next to impossible.

He gleefully threw my words back at me. "Is *this* distracting you?"

"Nope, not at all."

"I don't believe you."

"I'm just building up your anticipation for my final answer." I tried to collect myself, but it was difficult with the dual pleasure pushing me toward my climax.

Excited, he taunted, "What a load of bullshit. Admit it. You don't have an answer!"

"I absolutely do," I stubbornly insisted, even though I was still drawing a blank.

"Liar. Now you're the one who's stalling for time. But there's no point because there isn't an answer. That means I win by default!"

"No, my answer is so good, it'll blow your mind when you hear it," I bluffed.

He remained unconvinced. "In that case, enlighten me. Please share your genius answer so I can be amazed."

When I opened my mouth to reply, he played dirty by guiding me to take him deeper while pumping me hard. I gasped, the burst of white heat exploding through me so suddenly that it almost took me over the edge. Out of the corner of my eye, I caught sight of my clothes on the floor that gave me the words I needed for total victory.

"Last chance to answer for the win before I make you come so hard you forget the alphabet," he goaded me.

That wasn't an idle threat coming from him. However, my competitive need for victory helped me stay focused. "Zipper sex!"

He laughed incredulously. "What in the bloody hell is *zipper sex*, other than a phrase you just made up?"

"No, it's sex with your clothes on when you only

undo the zipper," I explained. "Ha, I fucking won! Suck it!"

"I'm not nearly flexible enough to do that in this position," he deadpanned, drawing an amused snort from me. "Consider me impressed and a little annoyed that you cheated by distracting me with your sexiness."

My laugh turned into a moan when he thrust deep. "You say as if you aren't equally or more distracting to me. I won fair and square."

"Congratulations on defeating me in the weirdest ABCs ever."

As I braced my hands on his chiseled abs, I loved how they flexed under me with every move we made. I traced the defined ridges, getting off on how built he was. The thought of my cum splattered over them, marking him as mine, was deeply appealing. I came hard, crying out his name as I did so. It was so intense that for a moment, I forgot how to breathe. I finally remembered to gasp for air, overwhelmed by the experience.

Ambrose grabbed my ass hard when he climaxed inside me. I loved being his and having him claim me in such a way. He sat up to kiss me, holding me close as he ravaged my mouth. I buried my fingers in his red hair and held on as he took everything from me I was willing to give.

When we separated for air, he teased me, "I love you, even when you kick my ass in a stupid game."

"Someone's got to keep that ego of yours in check."

He kissed me again, gentler this time. I melted against him with a contented sigh. There truly was no greater happiness than being loved by Ambrose and beating him in a challenge.

We both startled when his cell phone rang on the nightstand. It was his brother's ringtone, but I appreciated that he still asked, "Do you mind if I answer?"

"You should probably pull out of me first." He laughed as I moved off him to collapse on the bed.

He put it on speaker as he greeted his brother. "Hey, Cally. What's up?"

"Are you still at August's apartment?"

"Yeah. Do you need something picked up when I'm on my way home?"

There was a lengthy pause before Callum asked, "Um, no, but have you checked your messages recently?"

"No, I've had my phone set on do not disturb. Yours and Augie's numbers are the only two that can reach me when that's on. Let me check." He looked at his screen, wrinkling his brow in confusion. "All I have is a weird text from a number I don't recognize asking me if I'm home."

"Does it end in 4739?"

"Yeah. How did you know?"

Lost in my afterglow, I had no intention of paying attention to the conversation between the brothers until Callum answered, "It's Ma. She's on her way over here."

"*What*? Why? What the—fucking *what*?" He glanced at the message again. "That doesn't make sense! The text came from a local number."

"Ma got a prepaid SIM card like I did. But she accidentally bought a data-only one, so that's why she can only text," he explained. "She messaged me when she couldn't get ahold of you. She's on her way over from the airport."

"How is that even possible? Did she say why? Or for how long? What the fuck is going on?"

I wrapped my arms around Ambrose to hug him from behind, offering him what comfort I could. His mother had never visited America, so if she was here, something must have happened back home.

"I'm not sure. All she said was she was on her way and would see us soon."

"Look, we'll be there in like fifteen, twenty minutes. Call if you hear anything else from her, okay?"

They exchanged a few more words before hanging up. Ambrose got out of bed, then looked around my room in confusion. "Where the fuck are my fucking clothes?"

"Probably by the front door. You stripped out of them the second you walked in, remember?"

Despite his agitated state, he smirked at that. "It's not my fault. You're the one who answered the door naked and hard. My clothes never stood a chance at staying on."

I laughed as he left to retrieve them. When he came back, he told me, "You need to get ready, too. You're coming with me."

"But this is a family thing. If I'm there, she'll figure out I'm your boyfriend. You'll lose everything—"

He interrupted me. "She won't figure out you're my boyfriend. That's how I'm introducing you. I won't lose anything."

"How can you say that? Your father *disowned* Callum for being gay!"

"Right, Da did. Not Ma. She sent him to stay with me to keep him safe from Da, not because she was ashamed of Cally. If she's accepted him being gay, she'll accept me being bi."

"But what if she doesn't? You can't lose your mom." The possibility tore my heart apart. Having lost mine so young, I couldn't bear Ambrose having to endure that over his sexuality.

"Look, I don't know what's going on right now. But if Ma is here to see me and Cally, then she's chosen us over Da. Once she makes up her mind, absolutely nothing in this world will change it."

I tried to find humor in the situation. "Oh, so you get that from her? Good to know."

"Please come home with me, Augie. I want you

there with me for this, but I won't force you if you're uncomfortable with it."

"I'll go."

Ambrose gathered me into a tight hug. "Thank you."

I could have stayed in his embrace all day, but we had to go. For better or for worse, I was about to meet his mom. I trusted in Ambrose's certainty that this would be okay. The other thing that made me nervous was I had never been serious enough with anyone to meet their parents before. I hoped I wouldn't embarrass him in front of her. If she reacted badly, at least I'd be there to comfort him afterward.

Chapter Sixteen

AMBROSE

IT HAD BEEN three years since I had last been to Ireland and seen my family. When I had been grappling with my feelings for Augie, I had been too ashamed to go home. Once I had come to terms with how I felt for him, I had been scared they'd cut me off from my brother. It had been easier to remain in America.

But seeing my mother standing on my doorstep with four silver suitcases that were almost as tall as her, I regretted my decision to not visit. With her red hair styled in its customary braid, her fair skin and delicate features made her appear much younger than her years. Dressed in jeans and a black turtleneck, she was so petite that it was difficult to imagine that someone as massive as me could be her son. She may have been pint-sized, but she was one of the strongest people I had ever known.

"Ach, look at ye," Ma said in an awed voice. She gazed up at me with so much motherly pride in her warm blue eyes, it made it tough to speak around the lump in my throat. "Still such a handsome lad."

"It's so good to see you again, Ma." I reached out to hug her. She was so small and fragile in my muscular arms, but she smelled like home. A wave of nostalgia crashed over me as I held her. "I'm so sorry. I shouldn't have stayed away for so long."

She pulled back to smile up at me. "No, you did the right thing, Brody, much as it broke my heart not to see you."

I wanted to ask what she meant, but Callum came over. "Hi, Ma."

The tears that had gathered in her eyes fell as she looked at her youngest son. She hugged him with a sob. "Oh, Cally, I'm so sorry."

"It's okay," he reassured her, holding her as she cried.

"No, it isn't!" With trembling fingers, she brushed the edge of his fading black eye. "I should have fought for you harder, or—"

Callum interrupted her. "It's good we're here now."

Ma continued fussing over him as I brought in her four heavy suitcases. I couldn't imagine how my tiny mother had hauled so much luggage around when each of the bags weighed more than her. She was a light packer by nature, so the amount of baggage concerned me. "What's with all the luggage? Are you planning on moving in?"

She wiped the tear streaks from her cheeks with a laugh. "Heavens no. Two of them are for Cally, one of them is for you, and the other is mine."

"Really?"

"I figured none of us would be going back to that house for a long time, so I grabbed everything I could fit in those suitcases. It cost a fortune in overage fees, but money is about the only thing your worthless da is good for. Paying for it is the least he could do for trying to break up our family."

I understood why she had packed things for Callum since he had only brought a duffle bag with him. It touched me she did the same for me. After living abroad alone for almost ten years, I had forgotten how nice it was to have her take care of me. "Thanks, Ma."

She walked toward my living room, stopping when she saw Augie standing there. He looked gorgeous in his tailored black blazer, green shirt, and jeans, but his fidgeting fingers betrayed how nervous he was about meeting her. I was about to make introductions when she stopped me in my tracks by greeting him, "If it isn't Augie Murphy! How are you even prettier in person?"

While she had heard lots of stories and seen some pictures of him over the years, I had always referred to him as August. It was a mystery to me how she was aware of my nickname for him. I looked over at Callum. "Did you…?"

He shook his head. "I didn't tell her."

Augie held his hand out to her. "Um, hi. It's nice to meet you."

Instead of accepting the handshake, she embraced him. He hesitated before wrapping his arms around her in return. She leaned back to say, "I'll never be able to thank you enough for being a part of my son's life all these years. You've been a wonderful friend to him. I worried a little less knowing he had someone like you to rely on."

Ma hugged him again. Whatever she said for his ears only made his eyes go wide in shock. He looked dazed when she stepped back and sat down on the couch. What the hell had she said to him?

Callum took his place next to Ma, while Augie settled himself on the two-seater sofa next to it. I headed into the kitchen and started boiling water for tea. I grabbed four bottles of water and passed them out to everyone in the living room.

Ma gave me a disapproving stare. "Brody, I didn't fly all this way for water."

I sat down beside Augie, although it was a tight squeeze thanks to my broad build. "Don't worry, I already have the kettle on."

She leaned over to pat my knee. "What a good lad you are. No one can ever say I didn't raise you right."

"I'm thrilled you're here, but why the sudden trip?"

"Well, between you being bisexual and Cally being gay, I figured I'd give those old biddies at church a trifecta of gossip by divorcing that fucking piece of shite drunken arsehole I've had the misfortune of calling my husband for twenty-six years."

Her answer gave me whiplash from the amount of information I had to process. "Wait, you—" The kettle chose that very inopportune moment to interrupt. "Hold that thought."

I got up to prepare the tea, my head still reeling from her announcement. After adding cream and sugar, I brought a cup out for Ma and Callum first, before returning with one each for me and Augie. With that out of the way, I told her, "Let's start from the beginning. How the hell do you know I'm bi?"

She sipped her drink before responding. "Oh, I saw it on your Instatwitbook."

"Since when have you used social media?" I demanded.

Ma rolled her eyes at my question. "Why are you acting like I'm too old to know what that is?"

I bit back my urge to comment that she got the name of the websites wrong. It was true that I sometimes forgot how young Ma was. She had me at seventeen, so she was only forty-three and could still easily pass for being in her late twenties. Most people assumed she was my older sister rather than my mother. I was a fucking idiot for assuming she wouldn't see any of the posts I had made recently about being with my boyfriend.

"I loved your post about movie night. That picture Cally took of the two of you on the couch sharing a milkshake was adorable! It was wonderful to see the three of you so happy."

Augie blushed at the compliment. However, I was struggling to wrap my mind around the woman who had forced us to go to church and Catholic schools was suddenly fine with our sexuality. "Shouldn't you be condemning us to Hell for being sodomite sinners?"

She shook her head. "Da's the bigot, not me. If you're happy and your boyfriend treats you right, that's all I care about."

It was a fair point. Da had been the person espousing the most dogmatic ignorance and hatred in our house. She had always encouraged tolerance and acceptance, things he never had any use for.

"But you made us go to church!"

"No, Da forced you to go. I just rushed you in the morning to get there so we could hurry up and return home and be done with it. If I had my way, you never would have stepped one foot in a church. It's full of gossipy arseholes who preach hate and all think they're holier than thou. What a load of shite."

I rubbed my temples as I tried to process what she just said. "This doesn't make any sense."

"Why? I was raised by atheists. Your da is the religious zealot. I had no choice but to enforce it with you two to keep the peace, because nothing gets between him and Jesus except for alcohol and whores. He's such a fucking hypocrite."

"Also, since when do you curse?" I had only heard her say "fuck" once, and that was when she was crying alone on the stairs at our house, unaware I was there. It had haunted me for years.

That made her laugh. "Oh, please. I used to swear like a sailor until I met your da." It was rare to hear Ma talk about her life before him, so we knew next to nothing about her childhood. She had always insisted we didn't need to know about that and changed the subject.

Callum was the first to ask, "Really? But you never did it when we were growing up."

"It only takes getting hit once to learn that lesson. My goal was to ensure you boys never gave him a reason to do that."

My blood boiled at the thought of Da laying a hand on her. It made me want to get on the next flight to Ireland and take revenge for that and everything else he put us through. The only thing that calmed me was Augie's touch on my arm.

Ma took another sip of her tea before she continued. "You have to understand, when I met him, he wasn't like that. As someone who came from a family of abusive alcoholics, the salvation aspect of religion appealed to me. Your da wanted to save me from the heathens who raised me, and I was desperate to be saved. When I got pregnant, he thought it was a sign from God that he should marry me and start a family. I wanted away from my parents, so I agreed. The problems started later with the drinking."

I stared at her, struggling with the unsettling realization that I apparently didn't know her at all. "Why wouldn't you tell us?"

"Da didn't want you to know I came from a 'shameful family of unrepentant sinners.' It was a bleak period in my life that I wanted to forget, so it was easier to pretend it never happened. We both were happier that way."

"I'm sorry," I said, because I wasn't sure what words I could say to make that kind of hurt go away.

She reached over and stroked Callum's hair with a sorrowful expression. "No, I'm sorry I stayed so long and let him poison you with hate. But I had no family to turn to, no money of my own, and nowhere to go. All I could do was try my best to endure it and keep you safe. I turned a blind eye to his drinking and cheating, but I refuse to allow him to steal you two boys from me. He can choke on his sanctimonious sorrow as far as I care. It's time for the three of us to finally be happy without him."

Callum leaned over and hugged Ma with a sniffle. She soothed him, kissing his temple. I struggled with my own emotions and appreciated it when Augie wrapped his arms around me. "You can stay in my room as long as you want."

"Thanks, but I won't kick you and Augie out." I arched an eyebrow at her assumption he lived with me. It would take some time getting used to having that kind of support. "I'm staying at the Luxurian Hotel near here for a while. Later, I'll pop up to Portland to visit Siobhan and catch up with her."

Siobhan was Ma's closest friend who had moved to Oregon a few years ago with her husband for work. "That's good you can see her again."

Ma smiled beautifully as she agreed. "It is."

"Are you going to come back here after your visit with her?"

"No, I'll head back home to my new apartment your da will be paying for."

My eyebrows once again raised in surprise. "He agreed to that?"

The mischievous glint in my mother's eyes took me aback as she declared, "I'm not giving him any choice in the matter."

"But what if he refuses?" Callum asked, looking at her with concern.

"He won't." She said it with so much confidence that we had no choice but to believe her. "Anyway, enough of all that gloomy shite. I'm ravenous and want to hear about you three lads. What's for lunch?"

"Whatever you want." After the hell she went through for us with Da, I was ready to give her the sun, the moon, and the stars if that's what she asked for.

I HAD THOUGHT life couldn't get any better than being with Augie and Callum, but I was wrong. With Ma there, lighter and freer than I had ever seen her, everything was even more amazing. Without Da's overbearing and threatening presence, we could enjoy ourselves to the fullest. It blew my mind that she wholeheartedly embraced me and Callum despite our sexuality. She had doted on my boyfriend all night, making no secret of how much she adored him.

When I returned from dropping Ma off at her hotel, Augie and Callum were chatting in the living room. I sat on the sofa, gesturing for Augie to join me. When he tried to sit next to me, I pulled him onto my lap and wrapped my arms around him with a sigh that made him shiver. I rested my chin on his shoulder as I studied my younger brother. "How are you doing with everything?"

He rubbed the back of his head as he answered, "Honestly, I kind of feel like we're living in some parallel universe. I'm almost afraid we're going to wake up tomorrow and none of this will have actually happened."

I chuckled at the reaction. "Yeah, I know what

you mean. Never in a million years did I think Ma would react like that or leave Da."

"She's incredible," Augie said in awe. "I'm so happy for both of you."

I nuzzled against him, appreciating him saying that. "It makes me want to kill Da for what he's done to our family. We lost so many years of happiness because of him."

"The important thing is we have a fresh chance without him ruining everything." Callum always was the bright one. "We can finally be open and honest with each other, which is amazing."

"You're much better off focusing on the positives," Augie agreed. "Don't let that awful man steal your happiness from the present. He's taken enough."

I kissed his neck, making him tremble in my lap. It was giving me ideas about what I wanted to do with him once we were alone upstairs. "You're both right. But it's late, and today has been a long damn day. We should call it a night."

"Yeah, I could use the sleep," Callum said. "I still can't believe Ma's going to make breakfast for us tomorrow morning."

"Neither can I."

We exchanged a few more parting words before we went to our separate bedrooms. Once alone with Augie in mine, I embraced him tightly. "I'm glad you were here today."

"I am, too."

He let me hold him as long as I needed to. Ma's revelations had upended everything I had known about my life back in Ireland. It was a lot to process, but I drew strength from Augie's comfort and presence. "Jesus, Mary, and Joseph. What a fucking day."

That drew a laugh from Augie. "Your head must still be spinning from it all. Mine is, and I'm only dealing with my mistaken assumption that she would be a stern and humorless older woman. No wonder you're so damn handsome. She's stunning."

I stepped back and led Augie to sit together on my bed. "She always seemed older to me because of how unhappy she was. But seeing her so free tonight, laughing and joking like she didn't have a care in the world, it was weird realizing how young she actually is."

"Not to weird you out, but she seriously looks like your older sister and not your mom," he said with a sheepish grin. "Honestly, if she claimed to be twenty-eight, I'd believe her and still think she looks amazing for her age."

"People have been mistaking her for my sister my entire life. After seeing her tonight, I don't blame them. She was seventeen when she gave birth to me, so she's only forty-three now."

"That's incredible. It's obvious how much she loves the two of you."

I smiled at that. "She does, but she also adores you, too."

Augie hid his face against my shoulder with a sigh as I held him. It took him a while before he said, "She reminded me a lot of my mother. Even though I had fun tonight, part of me was sad that Mom never had the chance to know you like that. Our moms would have been lifelong friends, but they'll never meet."

"While I was never lucky enough to meet your mom, from the stories I've heard about her over the years, she was wonderful. Plus, she gave me you. I'll always love her for that."

His laugh bordered on a sob. "Shit, you're going to make me cry."

"It's okay to cry."

"But today was such a happy day," he protested.

"People also cry when they're happy."

He took a calming breath, steadying himself. I held him tighter as he snuggled against me. "More than anything, I'm so glad that the three of you can be a real family now."

"The four of us," I reminded him. "I told you before: you're part of our family, too."

Augie lost the battle with his tears as they fell. I kissed his forehead as we cuddled, blessed that he allowed me to love him. Once he had quieted to tiny sniffles, he surprised me by laughing.

"What's so funny?"

He sat up so he could meet my gaze. "I just realized that if I'm family, do I have to call you Brody now?"

"You can if you want to."

As if he were testing out the feel of the name on his tongue, Augie said, "Brody." He seemed pleased with the results. "Well, it would certainly be easier to moan during sex than Ambrose."

"How do you figure? They're both two syllables."

"Yeah, *technically*. But I rarely make it all the way through Ambrose, in case you haven't noticed. It usually turns into Ambro—*oh, god*!"

"Trust me, I've definitely noticed." It never failed to stroke my ego when it happened.

He moaned "Brody" to prove his point, stoking my lust. "See? It's shorter somehow."

The demonstration stirred my urge to make him moan my name for real. "Ambrose, Brody—I don't care, so long as it's my name you're crying out."

"Yeah, I'd imagine you'd have quite a few complaints if I called out Jimbo instead." We laughed at the absurdity of it. "It gives me something to look forward to later."

"Calling me Jimbo?"

"Oh, god no. Brody is *way* sexier than *Jimbo*."

While I had never considered my family nickname to be sexy, if anyone could make me reevaluate my opinion on that, it would be Augie. "Speaking of things that have nothing to do with that," I said, transitioning to an earlier issue that had been on my mind. "What did Ma say to you when she hugged you that second time?"

"She said, 'I hope Brody understands how lucky he is to have a boyfriend as cute as you,' which I didn't expect to hear," he answered. "You told me she didn't know you were bi, so it caught me off guard."

"Oh, I'm for sure the luckiest man on the planet to be with you. I also learned a very valuable lesson about using privacy settings online."

He snickered at that. "Sorry to break it to you, but you've lost that battle. Your mom followed me after she left, so she'll see it one way or the other."

I held in a sigh. "When we were in the car, she told me she was looking up her hotel reservation. Sorry, I can tell her to unfollow you tomorrow."

"Why?" He regarded me with a puzzled expression. "I already followed her back. Her posts are hilarious, plus her recipes are fantastic! I bookmarked a couple to try later."

Every time I thought I couldn't adore Augie more, he did things like that to make me fall in love with him all over again. I leaned over and kissed him. "You're amazing, you know that?"

"Your mom definitely thinks so," he retorted, causing us both to laugh again. "You're not so bad yourself. I think I'll keep you."

"Good, because I'm not going anywhere. I love you, Augie Murphy. So damn much."

"I love you, too, Brody Jimbo O'Rourke," he replied, barely able to contain his amusement.

"Yeah, yeah. Keep up the Jimbo stuff and I'll start

calling you Billy Bob Joe," I warned, which only made us crack up with more peals of laughter.

Tears of mirth gathered at the corners of Augie's beautiful green eyes. "You can't! That's way too difficult to moan mid-fuck."

I did it to prove him wrong, causing him to fall back onto the bed, his entire body shaking from laughing so hard.

Augie begged for mercy, which I very much enjoyed. "Stop, you're killing me! Poor Cally is probably trying to sleep." He held it together for about three seconds before he gasped out, "Billy Bob Joe," and broke into another fit of giggles.

I pinned him down on the bed, then started trailing kisses up his neck. When I neared his ear, I tugged on his earlobe, making him whimper. "By the time I'm done fucking you, you won't even remember your own name, Billy Bob Joe."

"No!" He shied away from me with a grumble that was more cute than threatening. "Don't you dare make that sexy!"

"Turnabout is fair play." I reached between us and cupped him through his pants, feeling victorious to discover he was already hard under my touch.

The fire in his eyes excited me when he challenged, "Do you *really* want to play that game with me right now? Because I will *so* kick your ass, Jimbo."

"I'd rather you fuck it, thanks," I replied, my prick stiffening with interest.

"Oh, you're on."

His sadistic glee aroused me. I'd be in so much trouble if he ever figured that out. Sexy, sexy trouble.

He was in the process of tugging off my gray sweater when a knock on my door caused us both to freeze. Callum called out from the other side, "Sorry, but where do you keep the toilet paper? The bathroom is almost out."

Damn it. I took a deep breath to compose myself before replying, "I'll come show you in a minute."

"Okay, thanks!"

Augie cupped my erection in his palm with an amused smirk. "Good luck hiding this monster from your brother."

His taunts added fuel to the lust burning inside me. "When I get back, your mouth is going to be too full to smart off." I thrusted against his hand so he knew exactly what I meant.

"Only if you're lucky."

I grinned. "That means it's guaranteed since we established earlier that I'm the luckiest man on the planet."

"I'm pretty sure that's me, actually." He gave me a tantalizing kiss, filling me with heat. "Hurry back, Brody. If you keep me waiting too long, I may have to introduce myself to Augusto."

The mental image of coming back to Augie fucking himself on my dildo was almost more than I could handle. That was an idea worth encouraging and seeing where it took us tonight. "Check the top drawer of the nightstand. He's light green, ten inches. You can't miss him."

"Why green?"

"There's three possible answers to that," I replied. "Your eyes made green my favorite color, I was green with envy that other people got to fuck you when I was dying to, or it was on sale. If you guess right, I'll give you something special when I come back." The real answer was all of the above, but that was for him to figure out.

The fire in his eyes when he ordered me to leave made it almost impossible to pull myself away from him. However, I forced myself to behave. Ignoring his snickers, I readjusted myself to hide my erection as best as I could. I left to take care of my brother's issue, eager to return to Augie's side and see what Augusto had in store for us that evening.

Chapter Seventeen

AUGIE

IT HAD BEEN three weeks since our trip to Las Vegas. In that time, I had learned what genuine happiness was thanks to my relationship with Ambrose becoming romantic. He was more than my best friend; he was the love of my life. I still couldn't believe my good fortune.

While Ambrose and I had hung out countless times with our friends Lucien and Rhys, I never imagined going on a double date with them. Then again, I never thought Rhys would elope with Lucien days before his wedding to his ex-fiancée, Olivia. I had been bitterly jealous back in Las Vegas that the two best friends had finally done something about their feelings for each other. But now that I had found the same happiness with Ambrose, I could be excited for them without being envious.

Sitting across from them in a booth at the Hurly-burly Bar and Grille, it was beautiful to see how in love they were with each other. At the same time, it amazed me at how little had changed in their dynamic.

Once we placed orders, Ambrose asked, "How's the married life treating you?"

"It was my best bad idea ever, right?" Rhys nudged his husband with a grin. Much like Ambrose dwarfed me, Rhys's lithe build was more noticeable because of how Lucien's broad frame. His lavender argyle sweater made his gray-blue eyes even more striking. "It's amazing, especially now that Luci is staying at my place while we find a new house together. I didn't know it was possible for life to be this good, but I'm grateful everything worked out for us."

"That makes two of us," Lucien said.

"How was your honeymoon?"

Lucien adjusted his glasses further up the bridge of his nose. "Shorter than we would have liked, but incredible. Greece is so beautiful it's hard to believe a place like that really exists on this earth."

It had always surprised me that as bookish as Lucien was, he had the chiseled body of an athlete. The tailoring of his black suit jacket and red button-down shirt enhanced his broad shoulders and defined muscles.

Both men were handsome, but I had only ever had eyes for Ambrose. I never tired of admiring his physical perfection that would put an ancient statue of a naked god to shame. He was extra gorgeous tonight in his blue V-neck shirt and jeans. With the sleeves pushed up, it showed off his impressive fore-arms. As good as he looked in that outfit, I was eager to see it on my floor after dinner. The thought distracted me so much that I almost missed hearing Rhys say, "If you ever get the chance, you should go. It's paradise."

"It sounds great." A vacation in paradise with Ambrose sounded heavenly. "The pictures you shared online were amazing."

"There were no filters or anything," Rhys told me. "The water is really that blue. It's unbelievable. But enough about us. What have you two been up to?"

"I have a situation that I could really use your help with," Ambrose replied.

"Do you need the number for one of our attor-neys?" Lucien joked, causing me to laugh. It was a fair question considering some of the scrapes we had gotten ourselves into back in college.

Ambrose grinned, but he quickly turned serious. "No, but I have a favor I'd like to ask, if that's okay."

"Wow, it must be serious if you're asking permis-sion," Rhys teased.

"It is, actually." Ambrose was normally full of jokes when the four of us got together, but Callum's predicament weighed heavily on his mind. "It's about my younger brother. Our dad threw him out when he found out Callum was gay, so he came to live with me last month."

Their faces reflected sympathetic concern. Lucien was the first to say, "Shit, that's awful. I'm really sorry to hear that."

"Your poor brother." Rhys shook his head. "I'm so sorry."

"Thanks. He's here on a tourist visa, but he has to go back to Ireland unless I can find a way to get him to stay here."

Without hesitation, Rhys volunteered, "I'm not sure how long it would take to make it happen, but if he's willing to work, one of us might be able to sponsor him for a work visa."

"You would probably have an easier time with that than me," Lucien told Rhys. It made sense given that Rhys owned a company that funded technology startups while Lucien ran a brokerage firm. "But if it isn't possible, we know enough people that someone should be in a position to help."

Ambrose was visibly relieved. "That would be amazing. Callum's twenty and inexperienced, but he's a hard worker and clever. If you tell him how to do something once, it'll be perfect. He's also meticulous with details."

I could see the wheels turning in Rhys's mind as he planned. "I've been pushing Xander too hard lately. Maybe your brother could be his assistant?"

Lucien arched an eyebrow. "You're getting your personal assistant an assistant?"

"Why not? Xander needs the help. Plus, it would be a good entry-level job. Callum could always transition into another role down the line once he's gotten some office experience."

"You're talking about that pretty boy we met in your honeymoon suite in Vegas, right?" Ambrose asked.

His description reminded me of the beautiful man we had run into when we went to visit Rhys and Lucien after finding out about their sudden marriage. I had burned with an ugly rage when Ambrose had checked him out, since Xander had been so gorgeous it made me self-conscious in comparison. It had been gratifying watching him blow off Ambrose. Few people could resist his charm—especially not me. "You mean the guy with the absurdly perfect eyebrows?"

"See? I told you I'm not the only one who notices Xander's eyebrows." Rhys elbowed Lucien. "They're so damn elegant it's weird. How do you not see that?"

The corner of Lucien's mouth turned up in a smirk. "If you say so." I got the sense that he was being deliberately obtuse to rile up Rhys. Some things never changed.

Rhys scowled at Lucien before returning his attention to Ambrose. "To answer your question, yes, that was Xander. Nobody works harder than him. He takes a lot of pride in doing his job perfectly, down to the smallest detail. If your brother can put up with that, I think it might be the best option."

"It sounds like a perfect fit. I don't know anybody who is more detail oriented than Callum."

"In that case, I'll talk to Xander about it tomorrow morning and have him get started on whatever needs done to secure a visa for Callum. If you could email me a copy of his passport and information soon, that would help."

Lucien asked in an amused voice, "You're going to make Xander do all the work to get his own assistant?"

"He's the person I trust the most to not fuck it up." Rhys shrugged. "If I want something done right, he's the guy who will get it taken care of. Plus, if Callum's going to be working for Xander, it makes sense for him to be involved in making that happen."

"Rhys, I can't thank you enough. I promise, Callum will be the hardest worker you have. You won't regret helping him. I'll send you everything when I get home tonight."

"I know firsthand how much it sucks to have your parents cut you out of their life because of who you love." Lucien reached over to caress the back of Rhys's neck to comfort him. The small gesture spoke volumes. "No one in my family has spoken to me since they found out we got married. I can only imagine how terrifying it would be to not only get kicked out of your home, but out of your country, especially when you're so young. Nobody should have to go through that. I don't know how fast I can make it happen, but I'm happy to do anything I can to help him out. And if I can't, I'll find someone else who can."

I squeezed Ambrose's hand under the table in silent support. "He's a good kid. He'll be okay."

"We'll make sure of it," Lucien promised.

"Sincerely, thank you."

With Callum's problem sorted, it was time for us to confess what had happened while the newlyweds were away on their honeymoon. I announced, "We also have some news to share with you guys."

"You hooked up in Vegas?" Lucien guessed.

Rhys stunned me with his guess. "Ooh, did you two elope, too?"

It came as a genuine surprise that both of our friends assumed that in one form or another, we had gotten together. "W-we didn't elope."

"Thought about it, but didn't," Ambrose added, causing me to stare at him with eyes wide in shock.

Completely forgetting we were in the middle of telling them about our relationship, I asked Ambrose, "You seriously thought about it?"

"Uh, well…" He shifted awkwardly on the bench with a rare blush on his cheeks. "I mean, kinda, yeah."

"How do you *kinda* think about eloping?"

He gestured at Lucien and Rhys. "It worked out great for them, so yeah, the thought crossed my mind. But——"

"But?"

"But now probably isn't the time to discuss that."

Rhys reacted before I had the chance to collect my thoughts. "Oh, that's a bullshit answer! You can't make him wait until later to find out what you were going to say. That's cruel."

While a large part of me echoed our friend's sentiment and appreciated him advocating for my interests, I also would hate being put on the spot like that if I was in Ambrose's position. "It's fine, you can tell me later."

I was prepared to table the topic to discuss after dinner in the car, but Ambrose stunned me when he explained himself. "The thing is, when I imagined our wedding, it was never us alone in a Vegas chapel. Felix and your dad were always a part of it. It wouldn't be right to do it without them there for you, no matter how ready I was to walk down the aisle with you."

The sentimental answer moved me almost to tears, which I had to fight back. I had already known from before that Ambrose had pictured us being married, but him respecting my family by making sure they could be there was everything to me.

I stared at him and struggled to find the right words to express what his answer meant to me.

Rhys once again beat me to the punch. "Damn, Ambrose. When did you get romantic?"

With hesitation, he answered, "When I fell in love with Augie."

"*Augie?*" Rhys looked over at Lucien. "How cute is that?"

"Adorable," Lucien deadpanned. The effect was ruined by his pleased smile. "Good for you, guys. It's about damn time."

That wasn't quite been the reaction I had been expecting. "It doesn't surprise either of you?"

"No, we've had our suspicions for a while. Although in fairness, Luci was clued in about you two way before me."

"That's because I identified with how August felt, even when I couldn't articulate it."

"We basically were in the same situation," I agreed, having found my voice.

Ambrose grinned as he asked Rhys, "Bet you never thought you'd have that in common with me, huh?"

"No, I really didn't." He picked up his drink and held up in a toast. "Here's to us getting our shit together to be with the greatest loves of our lives."

We clinked our glasses with cheers, then celebrated by kissing our partners. I never believed that day would come, but I was grateful things turned out that way.

WHEN WE GOT BACK to Ambrose's home after dinner with Lucien and Rhys, the first thing he did was email Rhys his brother's documents. Since Callum was still out with my brother, who I was pretty sure was officially his new best friend, I had assumed we would take advantage of the empty house once he finished. Ambrose surprised me by only wanting to snuggle in bed, spooning me with his massive body. It gave me a sense of comfort and protection on a primal level. Reality continued to be far superior to anything I had imagined over the years.

He was silent, which was unlike him. I asked, "Are you okay?"

"Mm-hmm." He hugged me tighter. "Better than okay."

"Why so quiet?"

It took him a moment to answer. "Just thinking."

"About?"

His answer was less than helpful. "Everything."

"Wow, that really narrows it down, thanks."

His chuckle sent a shiver down my spine. "I'm grateful that Rhys wants to help my brother. I'm thrilled Cally is becoming such good friends with Felix. That strawberry shortcake we had at the restaurant was incredible. You know, everything."

"Mm, it was delicious, wasn't it?" I shifted my

focus to Ambrose's primary concern. "Cally obviously didn't come here under great circumstances, but I think this is the best thing for him in the long run. He can be himself here in a way he couldn't be back in Ireland."

"I just want him to be happy."

"He is."

Silence fell between us once more. I almost thought he had fallen asleep until he continued. "Lucien and Rhys really love each other."

"They always have."

"It's odd. They're different now, but somehow the same." Ambrose nuzzled against me, making me smile. "I feel like we're the same way."

It was hard to articulate, but I understood. "I know what you mean."

"You're still my best friend, but you're so much more than that." His words made my heart swell with my affection for him. "I want what they have."

"But we have what they have. We're best friends who fell in love."

"Who go to their separate homes at the end of the night," he added. "The only thing harder than walking away from you is watching you leave."

The sentiment touched me. "That's sweet."

"I meant it when I told you that I would be satisfied with nothing less than all of you. It's selfish, but I want to keep you here with me."

"Then I'll stay here tonight. I don't think Cally will mind."

"Not just tonight. Tomorrow, and the day after that, and for the rest of our lives."

That conversation was too important to have without eye contact. I rolled over to face him. "Wait, are you asking me to move in with you?"

I wasn't used to seeing Ambrose's vulnerability, but it was on full display. "Yes, I am."

To say it surprised me would be a vast understatement. "Do you seriously want me to move in here?"

"More than anything."

I was overjoyed and ready to agree, but I still had to ask, "What about Cally?"

"He's fine with it."

That astounded me almost just as much as Ambrose's declaration about wanting me to move in had. "You talked to him about this already?"

"I did. He wants us to be happy, and being with you all the time makes me the happiest. Please move in with me, Augie."

How could I ever say no to that? "Okay."

Ambrose leaned closer and kissed me with the full force of his passion. I got swept away in the rush of emotions as my heart overflowed with love for my best friend and boyfriend. When we parted, I remembered what I had meant to discuss after dinner. "By the way, I wanted to thank you earlier."

He rubbed his thumb along my lower lip with a

smile. "Sorry, you kissed me stupid, darlin'. I have no idea what you're talking about."

I chuckled as his reaction. "What you said at dinner about wanting Dad and Felix to be there for our wedding. It meant a lot to me that you made that a priority because you knew how important that would be to me."

"It wouldn't feel right to get married if your dad wasn't there with Felix as your best man. All three of you would rightfully be mad at me for being selfish enough to elope."

I laughed at that. "The odds of Dad hunting you down would be pretty high."

He turned serious. "Augie, I want you to marry me because you want to, not just because it was a drunken Vegas whim."

With a raised eyebrow, I asked, "Is that a proposal?"

"No, not yet." He caressed the side of my face with a loving look. "I have big plans for that later, though."

"I don't know whether to be excited or terrified."

Ambrose chuckled at my reaction. "I'm still narrowing down my options, but I promise you'll love it when it happens."

"*Options*? As in plural?"

He grinned. "Why does that surprise you?"

"Because as many years as I've imagined being with you, I never once considered what it would be like if you proposed to me," I explained. "Mostly because it was so far beyond the realm of possibility that I couldn't even fathom it. Forgive me for being a little taken aback that you have fantasized about it enough to have a list of scenarios."

"What can I say? You inspired me to get in touch with my inner romantic."

Something warned me that side of him would have the tendency to go overboard. "Promise me one thing."

"Anything."

"Please don't let your inner romantic fill our bedroom with lit candles and rose petals all over the bed to seduce me. It'll give me anxiety about the fire hazard, the flowers will stick all over our sweaty bodies, and I refuse to clean them up when we're done."

It took a moment for him to rein in his laughter enough to reply, "You have my word. No lit candles, no rose petals, and no cleanup required from you."

"Hey, don't create a loophole. You deciding it's worth it to clean up yourself afterward doesn't make it okay. And don't do something stupid like substituting tulip petals because I only specified roses. I don't want flowers of any kind stuck on my ass, got it?"

Ambrose pretended to look disappointed. "Damn, there goes my plan for Saturday night. I sure hope the florist gives refunds."

"Brody!"

"Relax. The only thing that should be stuck on your arse is me," he replied, causing us both to laugh. "Damn it, that sounded way smoother in my head."

"It's a good thing you're hot," I teased him. His response was to reach over and caress my ass before groping it. "What are you doing? Checking to see if anything is stuck on it now?"

He gave me one of his most charming grins that immediately aroused my desire. "I may need to take a closer look, just to be sure."

"Go for it." I loved giving myself over to him as he pleasured me beyond my wildest fantasies. It was a dream come true that I had managed the impossible by turning my fake boyfriend for one night into my partner for forever.

Epilogue

AMBROSE

ONE MONTH LATER

I LOOSENED my tie as soon as I got home after a hellacious day at work. Everything had gone wrong at the office, but my frustrations faded at the smell of something delicious cooking in the kitchen. I followed the scent, leading me to Augie cutting vegetables while two pots bubbled on the stove. He wore an apron over his blue-and-white pinstripe shirt and tight jeans that made his arse look fantastic. The domestic scene filled me with joy, making me forget all about my shite day.

Even though he had only moved in two weeks ago, the novelty of coming home to him hadn't worn off yet. Hugging Augie from behind, I nuzzled against him as I relaxed for the first time since I had left that morning. "Hi, darlin'."

Augie tilted his head to give me a kiss I savored. "Welcome home." He returned his attention to chopping a bell pepper, but I refused to let go to make it easier for him to work. Instead, I started trailing kisses along his neck. "Isn't this the part of your fantasy when I'm supposed to threaten you with bodily harm if you don't stop distracting me?"

I chuckled at the reminder of the scenario I had shared with him about fending off my attention while cooking. "You can, but it won't deter me." I traced the shell of his ear with my tongue before tugging on it with my teeth. My actions earned me a breathy moan that gave my prick sexy ideas. "You're irresistible."

"So you say." His tone was laced with amusement as he stirred the white sauce and then the boiling pasta.

"Are you inviting me to show you how tempting you are?"

"On the kitchen counter?" He added the peppers to a pan with other vegetables and began to sauté them.

I laughed. "You know me so well."

"You'll have to wait for another night. Ma, Dad, Felix, and Cally are on their way over for dinner, remember?"

Unable to resist temptation, I slipped my hand under his apron to grope him through his pants. "Come on, we've got time to squeeze in a quickie."

"As I recall, you were quite insistent that there were no sex words that started with the letter *Q*."

"Yes, and then you taught me a very sexy lesson I enjoyed learning." I tried and failed to undo the button of his jeans. "Let me prove what an excellent student I am."

He nudged me back. "No, I'm not burning dinner and embarrassing myself tonight. This is one of Ma's recipes, so I can't fuck it up."

I never tired of hearing Augie calling her Ma as if she was his own mother. It was touching to see how close they had become in such a short amount of time.

He dipped the wooden stirring spoon in the sauce to stir it, before bringing it up to me. "Does it taste right?"

"It tastes just like hers. They'll love it."

"Hopefully. The chicken is seasoned and just needs put in the oven," he told me. "I didn't want to leave it in too long and dry it out, but they'll be here soon."

I kissed his cheek. "I'll go change real quick so I can help."

"Thank you, that would be great."

Not wanting Augie to do everything by himself, I hurried to get ready. When I returned, we worked as a team to do the last preparations for the meal.

After I set the table, he gestured for me to come

closer. He guided me down for a sweet, lingering kiss. "I love you, in spite of the fact that you almost made me ruin my sauce."

"I would still love you even if you burned dinner."

He laughed. "Wow, I'm so glad to know our relationship isn't at risk from culinary disasters."

"Nothing could ever stop me from loving you, Augie."

"I feel the same way about you."

My heart sang as we kissed again. Life was beautiful because my best friend, my boyfriend, my future husband loved me.

Which unexpected guest surprises Ambrose and Augie on their first anniversary celebration at a cabin? **Claim your copy of Mighty Cute to find out who**.

Do you want to see adorable Callum get the happily ever after he deserves? **Read Fancy Love next to enjoy a sugary sweet and steamy romance**.

Curious to see where Ambrose and Augie's story begins? **Check out Bet on Love today**.

Thank You

Thank you for reading **Love Means More**. Reviews are crucial for helping other readers discover new books to enjoy. If you want to share your love for Ambrose and Augie, please **leave a review**. I'd really appreciate it!

Recommending my work to others is also a huge help. Don't hesitate to give this book a shout-out in your favorite book rec group to spread the word.

About the Series

The good news is that if you loved Ambrose and Augie and can't wait to see more of them, you can read an exclusive bonus chapter of their first anniversary celebration if you join my newsletter.

Did you think Ambrose's younger brother, Callum, was a sweetheart in need of a happily ever after of his own? Then don't miss the next book in this series, **Fancy Love**. Callum gets set up on a blind date with Rune Tourneau, a jaded model who doesn't believe in true love. Rune becomes captivated by Callum's sweet, sunny disposition, and starts to feel things for the younger man he never expected. It's a sweet and heartfelt story, featuring a grumpy/sunshine, age gap, first time, opposites attract, gay romance. This feel-good story will have you cooing from how adorable it is and fanning yourself from the heat.

The good news is that Ambrose and Augie both appear in that book, as well as Rhys from **Bet on Love**. If this book is your introduction to the **Good Bad Idea** series, I'd definitely recommend checking that one out to see where all the fun begins.

Don't worry, I didn't forget about Augie's younger brother, Felix! He's too awesome not to have his own story, so you'll definitely want to check out the sixth book in the series, **Picture Love**. It features his romance with his friend Izzy's older brother, Arsène. The two of them have fiery chemistry with smoking hot steam coming off the pages as they engage in sexy banter. It's a hilarious brother's best friend, insta love, age gap, gay romance you definitely won't want to miss!

Felix's friends Wren and Izzy will also have their chance to find love together in the seventh book in the series, **Love Practice**. It's a friends to lovers, room-mates, fake dating, gay romance that will have you rolling with laughter.

To stay up to date on the latest series news, please be sure to subscribe to my newsletter for access to bonus chapters. You can also join my Facebook group, Ariella Zoelle's Sunnyside, where I post exclusive weekly teasers. I'm also on Twitter and Instagram.

Next in Series

AVAILABLE NOW

Rune has become jaded by his shallow life as a fashion model. But when he meets a ray of sunshine named Callum, he rediscovers joy. Can the unlikely couple find true love together?

Callum O'Rourke

As a very shy and sheltered twenty-year-old who is just starting to live my truth for the first time, I have a *lot* to learn about being gay. When I meet Rune, I discover dreams really do come true and my perfect partner exists for real. How can I not fall for him when he's older, gorgeous, loves baking, and nerds out about history the same way I do? Even though I'm lucky enough to become his friend, I can't stop myself from wanting to be more. I know pushing for anything else would be foolish, but I can't stop wishing my first time would be with him.

I want to experience *everything* about being loved by a man. Could I really be bold enough to ask him to be my teacher?

Rune Tourneau

Life had lost all of its luster and became a monochromatic blur of meaningless encounters with strangers. But when Callum appears, his warmth explodes my world into a vibrant technicolor dream I never want to wake up from. Like a breath of fresh air, he brings joy and laughter to my heart once more by being a ray of sunshine to brighten my darkest days and makes me want to be his for good.

My inner cynic swears this is a bad idea because Callum is too good, too pure, too sweet, and too young to end up with an older, jaded guy like me who always thought true love was a lie. But he makes me want to believe in a happily ever after.

If we can possibly write our own fairy tale romance together, isn't it worth taking a chance on love?

Fancy Love is the third book in the ***Good Bad Idea*** series and part of the Sunnyside universe. This novel features a grumpy/sunshine, age gap, first time, opposites attract, gay romance. If you love cute sweetness, sexy fun, and low angst stories that will make you laugh and swoon, you'll adore this satisfying HEA without cliffhangers. Each book can be read as a standalone or as part of the series in order.

Also by Ariella Zoelle

For a complete and up-to-date list of Ariella Zoelle's low angst releases, please visit her website at

www.ariellazoelle.com/ariella-zoelle-all

Also by A.F. Zoelle

In the mood for something with more angst and drama?
Check out A.F. Zoelle's dark romances at

www.ariellazoelle.com/af-zoelle-all

Acknowledgments

There aren't enough words for how grateful I am to everyone for the overwhelming support this **Good Bad Idea** series has received! The positive and enthusiastic reaction was beyond my wildest dreams. I'm so happy everyone enjoys it so much. This series will be a fun ride, so I'm very grateful for everyone wanting to come along on the journey together.

I'm also grateful to Mona, Taylor, and Zelda-Marie for all of their kind encouragement as I've worked on this project! They are all such special people near and dear my heart. It's wonderful being able to share in the joy of this project with them.

A special thank you goes to Cate, Pam, and Sandra for all of their amazing help in putting this together. It's been a dream working with them and I'm appreciative of their help and guidance.

I'm also grateful to Katie from Gay Romance Reviews and all of the ARC readers who made *Bet on Love* such a great success! I loved hearing all the reactions to it, so thank you to everyone who took the time to leave a review.

Let's meet again in **Fancy Love**!

About the Author

ariella zoelle

WWW.ARIELLAZOELLE.COM

Ariella Zoelle adores steamy, funny, swoony romances where couples are allowed to just be happy. She writes low angst stories full of heat, humor, and heart. But sometimes she's in the mood for something with a bit more angst and drama. If you are too, check out her A.F. Zoelle books.

Get a bonus chapter by using the QR code below!

Made in the USA
Las Vegas, NV
16 May 2024

89952461R00118